TAKE FIVE

SHORT STORIES

DOUGLAS CLARK

Cover photograph and contributing design by Lauralee McKay
Dreams New York photograph by Lauralee McKay
Situation Room White House photograph by Keith Stanley

This book is a work of fiction. Any resemblance to actual events or persons, living or dead, is entirely coincidental.

"Take Five," by Douglas Clark. ISBN 1-58939-784-3 (softcover); 1-58939-797-5 (hardcover).

Published 2005 by Virtualbookworm.com Publishing Inc., P.O. Box 9949, College Station, TX 77842, US. ©2005, Douglas Clark. All rights reserved. No part of this publication may be reproduced, stored in a retrieval system, or transmitted in any form or by any means, electronic, mechanical, recording or otherwise, without the prior written permission of Douglas Clark.

Manufactured in the United States of America.

Dedicated to Josie, whose unfailing enthusiasm and editing contributions brought *Take Five* to print.

Also by Douglas Clark

BELFAST, A Novel of the Troubles

TAKE FIVE

By Douglas Clark

"Is all that we see or seem but a dream within a dream?"
Edgar Allen Poe, A Dream Within a Dream

Gordon Blanchard was shown into the Controller's office.

"Mister Blanchard, your message was somewhat cryptic. May I ask why you are coming directly to me rather than to Chuck Haley?" Fred Morrison asked.

"Sir, with all due respect to Chuck, I thought the fewer people who know about this....this information, the better," Blanchard answered. Blanchard was a senior internal auditor for Global Resources & Logistics, GRL, a large multi-national company. Chuck Haley was his boss who reported to Morrison the company controller.

"Very well, Mister Blanchard, what have you got to tell me?"

"It's about Caspian, Sir. I'm afraid there is the likely possibility that serious fraud and corruption is going on. Probably for some time. Years. I have----"

Morrison cut him off, "What the hell are you talking about, Blanchard?"

"I am suggesting that there is evidence of fraud, money laundering, and probably bribery involving Caspian Enterprises."

Blanchard went on to explain that he had been at Caspian Enterprises corporate headquarters in Moscow for two weeks, followed by another three weeks probing deeper into various suspect areas he unearthed.

"What specifically are you saying you've found?" Morrison asked.

Blanchard paused to organize what he wanted to say. Like any exec, Morrison did not like a problem thrown into his lap. "In brief, Sir, Caspian is selling gas, oil, and electrical power at well above market prices to all sorts of government entities across the former Soviet Union states. There are poorly documented outflows of large sums that I believe are probably bribes. More disturbing even than that is the buy side. As you know, Caspian leases all manner of transportation equipment and services. Many of these leases are with companies that are merely shells. Frankly, I believe they are vehicles for laundering drug money."

Morrison was visibly in distress. "Christ, Blanchard, you know how things are over there. Markets are more volatile, the controls are loose. Documentation is inherently poor."

"I understand what you're saying, Sir, but I've gone beyond that in several lines of investigation. There are major gaps, inconsistencies, and outright areas that cannot be explained with documentation. Frankly, the outside auditors have been sleeping or they would have latched onto the same things I found."

"Do you have evidence as to who is involved?" Morrison asked as he hunched over his desk leaning towards Blanchard.

"Not specifically, but the scope suggests it must be senior executives at Caspian. I understand that Caspian was formed from three acquisitions a few years ago. The former Russian principles are still the senior management. They have to be in on this. This could drag down Global just like Enron."

"I have written a detailed report with supporting documentation as addendums. It's all here on this CD, Sir." Blanchard said and handed the CD to Morrison. "Management needs to act quickly on this. If they go about it right, they can eliminate the problem quietly, or at least downplay Global's involvement. After all, it's the Russians not the U.S. that got screwed."

Morrison was dumbfounded. Finding his voice he said, "I can't agree with your conclusions until I have studied your report. Give me a couple of days and I'll get back to you. If I concur, I'll kick this up to the boss. In the meantime, don't discuss this with anyone. Not Haley, not your wife, not anyone. Even if you're dead wrong, this sort of thing can cause a volcano on Wall Street."

"No problem, Sir. That's why I brought it to you."

Blanchard left Morrison's office.

Morrison called the office of the Chief Financial Officer for Global, William Ryder. "I don't give a damn if he's in a meeting, put me through immediately," Morrison yelled at Ryder's secretary.

Three days after his meeting with Morrison, Blanchard still had not heard from him. Repeated calls and a visit to Morrison's office were unsuccessful. The following morning he left for Los Angeles on a new assignment. For the next two weeks he was part of a team doing due diligence for a possible acquisition.

There was still no word from Morrison, two days into his work in Los Angeles. The brass were probably still struggling with how to manage the crisis. Probably were pursuing some sort of verification. Probably just didn't know whether to shit or go blind. Fuck'em. If they're too stupid to act on his investigation, then there's nothing more he can do. He did his job. His ass was covered.

Day three in sunny Los Angeles was anything but sunny. Neither were the first two days here. It was early June. *June gloom* the locals called it. Gray mornings with a fair amount of fog mixed with the usual pollutants. It was supposed to 'burn-off' at mid-day, but sometimes not.

Blanchard had set a small morning routine. It was a five-block walk to the investment banking office where he was working. There was a non-franchise coffee shop with a couple of seats outside. It was reasonably chilly at seven AM, so he was the only one sitting outside. Cappuccino, a scone, and the New York Times.

A large SUV accelerated from a parked location two blocks away. Blanchard had his back to the vehicle as it approached along with only modest traffic at this early hour. Close to the coffee shop, the vehicle veered onto the sidewalk.

Blanchard was struck from behind, the impact hurling him through the plate glass window of the coffee shop, The SUV reversed, then sped off.

Carol Simmons had been coming to the UCLA Medical Center in Santa Monica, California every day for the past week to visit her brother Gordon Blanchard. She and Gordon were not close, but they were the only family either had. She was in Dr. Edward's office, the neurosurgeon treating her brother.

"Miss Simmons, your brother has been in a coma since the accident. I am amazed that he survived this trauma. Still, we're hopeful that he will regain consciousness. We think there is good reason to be hopeful that will happen. However, you can well imagine the emotional issues he will suffer."

Carol Simmons knew full well the extent of her brother's injuries. Paralysis from the waist down with no possibility of recovery because of the extent of his spinal injuries. Loss of his right arm. Loss of his right eye. Substantial disfigurement to his face. She was told that even with extensive reconstructive surgery, his appearance might still be disturbing.

"I understand he's not married. No known girlfriend. Your parents are deceased. He's from New York. No friends out here on the West Coast. You would seem to be his only intimate contact. He'll especially need your support, and probably professional help."

Gordon Blanchard regained consciousness the following night. His moaning alerted a nurse. He would have screamed had he been able.

After an examination by the shift resident, a strong sedative allowed him to return to sleep for the remainder of the night. The next morning his sister was at his bedside.

"Jesus, Gordon. I don't know what to say. I'm so sorry to see you like this."

Blanchard struggled to move his damaged face to form speech. It came out barely distinguishable.

"The doctor told me how bad I am. Never going to walk he said."

His sister struggled with tears. "Gordon, it's too early to make those judgments. You've just come out of a coma. Don't despair. We'll get other opinions. Just try to get your strength back now."

"The driver? Who?" Blanchard asked.

His sister answered, "The police don't know. It was a hit and run. They have not been able to locate the vehicle."

"How long have I been unconscious?"

"Gordon, you've been in a coma for over a week. We weren't sure you would even live."

Blanchard struggled to stay awake. "GRL? Anyone from GRL been around?"

"I don't know. There's flowers here from your company, though," his sister said.

A nurse entered the room. "Miss, I'm afraid the patient needs to rest. The doctor said to limit your visit to only a few minutes. You can see him again tomorrow."

Blanchard's sister told him to rest and she would be back tomorrow. She wanted to kiss him, but didn't know where. She left after a gentle squeeze to his hand.

Blanchard eyes fluttered and he lapsed into a sedated sleep.

He woke in the early morning. Sunlight was evident through the cracks of the window blinds. The remains of his dream were still with him. He had dreamt he was back at the Caspian offices in Moscow. He was walking. He was whole.

His sister visited again midday.

"Anything further from the police, Carol?" he asked.

"No. I don't think they hold out much hope. The detective suggested that the vehicle has probably been repaired by now," she answered.

"I don't think it was an accident, Carol."

His sister was not sure she heard him correctly. "What do'ya mean?"

"I discovered some things when I was in Russia. Major things going on at Caspian. Things that could destroy

GRL if they became public. It would be worse than En-ron."

"What sort of things?" she asked.

"Corruption. Criminal stuff. It's very technical. I want you to get my laptop from the hotel."

His sister paused for several moments. "I got your clothes and stuff from your hotel room. The police helped me. But ---- but there was no laptop in the room."

Gordon Blanchard just groaned and mumbled, "Shit." He was defeated. It was them. He had no evidence and he was a cripple.

"Carol. Call the nurse. The pain's real bad. I need a shot."

The nurse injected morphine into his IV. He said goodbye to his sister and drifted into sleep within minutes.

. . . .

I left my Moscow hotel and got into the old Mercedes that picked me up every morning. "Good morning, Igor," I said to my driver. I smiled thinking of the Marty Feldman character in Young Frankenstein with the name pronounced *Eye-gor.* It was October. Cold and gray, but no snow yet. Moscow would look better with a blanket of snow. Now she looked like a whore without her makeup in the morning.

Caspian Enterprises corporate offices were located in a fashionable business district on Chistoprudny Boulevard. I arrived at the small office I had been given for this audit assignment at Global's Moscow subsidiary, and unlocked the door.

The office gopher girl brought me a coffee. "Helga, where are all the files I had on this table?"

"I do not know, Sir. You keep door locked, do you not?" she answered.

I was a little confused. I remembered leaving stacks of files on the table adjacent to the desk. Today I had planned on probing business transactions with a firm known as Eurasian Consulting. I had pulled a number of contracts with EC that I intended to research, but now they weren't here. In fact, the office was clear of everything except the telephone. Things just weren't right.

As I was booting my laptop, a striking woman opened the door. "Mister Blanchard? I am Irina Petrenko from the Information Technology Department. I was instructed to assist you in your work."

Instructed by whom? He did not remember requesting specific computer help. Wonderful however. It was hard to take his eyes off Ms. Petrenko. "Thank you, Ms. Petrenko. Maybe later I will have something you might help me with. Right know I need to locate certain contracts. Where would those files be?"

"The originals would be in Contracts Administration. However, it will be much quicker to access them on the computer. Everything is scanned and filed electronically. Much easier to provide wide access and still maintain proper security."

"What about receipts and payment voucher authorizations? Where are those hard copies kept? Blanchard asked Petrenko.

"Hard copies? You mean paper copies? Most are also electronic. We have electronic signature capability to our system. I will explain all details if you like. Please to come to my office and I will assist your search. I am told by my superior you have highest access security." She said.

What seemed like at least a pleasing collaboration, turned out also to be productive. In what seemed like no time, I had enough information on two contracts to raise suspicions.

"How long your visit to Moscow, Mister Blanchard?"

"Well, Miss Petrenko...." but she interrupted with "You may call me, Irina."

"Excellent. And you may call me Gordon. I will be here for a few weeks."

"Perhaps you would like to join me and some friends for a drink after work? We could get something simple for dinner later."

I easily accepted. Irina was not only pretty, but smart and talented. I couldn't remember the last time I had a real date.

Close to midnight I found myself helping Irina out of the taxi at her apartment building. She was still laughing and navigating poorly with all the vodka we had consumed. Curiously, I was not feeling drunk myself though. Fortunately, Irina's flat was only on the third floor since there was no elevator.

"Come in for a drink, Gordon," Irina said slurring the words slightly.

"It's pretty late, Irina. We both have to be at work in the morning."

"How do you say, *to hell with it*. No, *fuck it*!" she said. "See I know American slang good," she said. She closed the door and threw her arms around my neck. Her body pressed hard against me and she kissed me hungrily with her mouth open.

We pulled off our clothing and quickly moved to the bedroom. The lights were fully on. Her magnificent body captivated me as I entered her.

Irina lay asleep next to me on the narrow bed. I remembered feeling the sensation of being inside her, but not of climaxing. Something like the missing pieces in a dream. Probably all the vodka I drank. I was also sleepy and soon drifted into unconsciousness.

. . . .

"Mister Blanchard, time to bathe you," the nurse said. With the aid of a large male orderly, his unresponsive body was elevated onto its left side. He could do nothing but tolerate the indignity of the nurse sponge-washing his back and butt. Worse yet, when she washed his genitals. Blanchard could see, but not feel any sensation.

Recalling the dream for the next several hours gave Blanchard alternating thoughts of pleasure and utter despair. Lovemaking would never be part of his future.

The next dose of pain narcotic lapsed him into sleep.

■ ■ ■ ■ ■ ■ ■ ■ ■ ■

I woke to the smell of coffee. Irina brought two mugs into the bedroom. She was completely and gloriously naked. "Drink your coffee quickly. We must shower. To save time, we shower together, but washing is all we have time for. You must wait till later for other," she said with a grin.

"How do we get to the office?" I said as we dressed.

"Bus of course," she answered.

"I have a car that picks me up at my hotel. Should we call the hotel?"

Irina said, "I call hotel. Have them tell driver he is not needed this morning. We take bus. Will not raise eyebrows? Is that correct way to say?" Irina said.

I would not have minded being late after the delight of touching Irina's body in the shower, but she insisted that at least she must be on time.

I went to my assigned office. Irina had given me enough of an understanding of the system, but only the international documentation was in English. Intra-country material was in Russian. The Cyrillic alphabet made it even more difficult to recognize key business terms.

Vadim Sorokin, Caspian's head of operations had an office as well appointed as any Wall Street investment banker. From a large window, there was a panoramic view of the old part of Moscow. "Come in Mister Blanchard," he said as his secretary showed me in. "Will you take a coffee with me?"

"No thank you, Sir"

"Please be seated and tell me what I can do for you."

"Well, Sir, it would make my audit much easier if I could have someone assist me in areas of interpretation."

"Has Miss Petrenko not been helpful?"

"Oh no. Quite the opposite. She has been enormously helpful. She is very knowledgeable and efficient. It's in the area of language where the documentation is in Russian that I could use some help."

Sorokin dropped his smile and looked at me with some intensity. "But are not all our accounting documents and systems in English?"

"Yes they are. However, most documents involving transactions with Russian companies, and even with Ukrainian and Georgian firms, are in Russian."

It was impossible for Blanchard to get even a few repetitive words understood with the Cyrillic alphabet. Words looked like hieroglyphics.

"I can see you are thorough in your work. What do you need to assist you?" Sorokin asked.

"That's easy. Perhaps you could spare more of Miss Petrenko's time. Since she knows the computer system, if she could also assist in locating and translating supporting information, it would be of great assistance."

"Very well, Mister Blanchard. Let me see what I can arrange," Sorokin said.

After lunch, Irina came into his office.

"Mister Sorokin said I was to provide you with whatever assistance you required," she said.

Blanchard smiled at what he thought was the innuendo, but Irina was not smiling. She closed the door.

Irina sat down and looked serious. "What is it you are doing, Gordon?"

"What do you mean? I'm auditing the books. I need to verify transactions by reviewing the supporting documents. I need help with those documents that are in Russian. You can translate for me."

"I will do my best, Gordon," she said. "Do you wish me to do certain work now?"

I was slightly hurt by her seemingly coolness, but got down to the work at hand. "Let's start with this company called Krasny & Belopolsky. The general ledger account identifies them as a consulting firm. I need to see their contract and invoices for the last twelve months."

Irina returned in what seemed a short time with a pile of papers and sat down next to him.

"I made copies for you," she said. "Tell me what you wish to know."

"Start with the contract. What do they do and what is in the contract?"

"They are to assist in securing orders from government offices for energy."

"What kind of energy?"

"All types, gas, petroleum, coal."

"And how are they paid?"

"The contract lists many pages of services and fees. Some work is paid by how much time Krasny & Belopolsky staff work for Caspian, others are commissions."

"How much business did Caspian do with Krasny & Belopolsky last year?"

Irina thumbed through several printouts. "One hundred seventy-five million."

"Rubles?" I asked.

"No, dollars. United States dollars.

I was dumbfounded. $175 million dollars in consulting fees and commissions!

I worked with Irina for the rest of the afternoon, or at least I thought I did. The time went by without recollection and now it was nighttime. I was alone again with Irina.

"What are you looking for, Gordon?"

"I wasn't looking for anything, but I think I've found some irregularities."

"Irregularities? What does that term mean?"

"Things that are not right. Maybe even illegal," I answered.

Irina was quiet for a few moments, then said, "Mister Sorokin asked me to report to him about all the files you request. He ordered me not to tell you. But I do not like Mister Sorokin. He is unsavory. He wants to, how you say, get into my pants. He is a pig."

. . . .

Blanchard woke. His sister was at his bedside.

"How are you feeling this morning, Gordon?" she asked.

It was an innocent remark, but still a dumb fucking question. He would never feel 'good ' any morning for as long as he lives. He was not reconciled to his fate. He was not motivated to overcome his disabilities. Given the means, he would gladly end his life.

Blanchard had improved his speech capability slightly. "Carol, it was no accident. Someone tried to kill me. It was because of what I found out in Russia. There's huge corruption at Global's subsidiary, Caspian Enterprises.

"Gordon, you don't know that this was anything other than an accident. Regardless, you must now concern yourself with getting well," his sister said.

"Getting well? They destroyed me. I'll be a cripple for life. I'm disfigured. When I dream, I'm whole. I can walk. Then I wake to reality. It would have been better had I been killed."

For the remainder of her visit, his sister tried to dissuade him from his depressed thoughts. If he were to have had any mobility, she would have worried about suicide. She ended by suggesting he needed to talk with someone *professional* because his depression would certainly inhibit his recovery.

As much as he appreciated his sister's love, he tired of her motherly advice. He was anxious to return to his dreams. He pleaded discomfort with the pain. Minutes later, the duty nurse injected the narcotic into his IV tube and he drifted off within moments.

■ ■ ■ ■ ■ ■ ■ ■ ■ ■

I found myself walking down the hall and turning into my office at Corporate in New York City. How I suddenly found myself back on this side of the Atlantic was not clear. I really wanted to see Irina. It was morning in Moscow. With some maneuvering through international operators I got through to Caspian Enterprises and asked for Irina Petrenko in the computer section. A male voice answered in Russian. I identified myself and asked for Irina.

"Mister Blanchard, you must not know? Miss Petrenko was killed two days ago. It was terrible. All here at office are upset and mourn very much," the man said.

I could hardly speak. "What happened?"

"She was struck by large truck when she cross street. People who saw accident say truck drove off after striking her. Did not even try to help poor Irina."

I hung up the telephone and cried. I walked through the near empty offices of Global Resources & Logistics. It was seven o'clock in the evening in New York. I got to Fred Morrison's office and went right in since his door was open and his secretary was gone for the day.

"Do you have a few minutes, Mister Morrison? I have something urgent."

"I guess so, Blanchard. Have a seat." I closed the door but did not sit down.

"I've discovered irregularities during my audit of Caspian. I'm working on my report, but this cannot wait now."

I had Morrison's attention, "What do you mean irregularities?"

"Fraud, money laundering, bribery, and maybe now, murder," I answered.

"Jesus Christ, murder? What the hell are you talking about, Blanchard?"

"It involves leases, subcontractors, consulting companies. Caspian executives Nikolai Melnikov and Konstantin Yudin are clearly implicated. I've got evidence that could get them indicted. They weren't even clever about disguising the transactions. My predecessor was either bought off or he was an idiot."

"I'll need to see your report and the evidence, Blanchard," Morrison said.

"No fucking way! You must act on this right away – Sir."

"What's got into you, Blanchard? I can't do anything without evidence."

"Listen, Sir. They apparently know what I found. They'll start to cover their tracks and destroy evidence. Take it to the CEO. Isolate these assholes and secure our records."

"Christ Almighty, Blanchard, you sound like a lunatic. I'm not taking anything all the way to Albright on your say so. You haven't shown me shit."

"Sir, I know it's urgent because a woman I worked with over there was just murdered. It's because she helped me and knew too much."

"Murdered? How was she murdered?"

"Struck down by a truck. Hit and run."

"Jesus, Blanchard. How in the hell do you know it was murder?" He came around the desk and put his hand on my shoulder. "Listen, I can see why you're upset. Put your report and evidence together as quickly as you can and I'll get it up to at least Volkoff. Volkoff supervised the acquisitions that formed Caspian and he'll know what to do. But I need more than your accusations."

I left his office and he closed his door. As I walked past his secretary's desk I noticed the light on her telephone indicate that Morrison was making a call. I carefully lifted the receiver and shielded the mouthpiece to listen in.

"----I don't know what he's discovered Mister Volkoff, but he seems convinced it's compelling evidence. What would you like me to do, Sir?" Morrison asked.

The man on the other end of the call said, "Nothing. Obviously keep a close eye on this Blanchard fellow. Certainly don't confide in anyone about his allegations. If he gets his materials together and gives them to you, call me immediately. It's important that you contain this, Morrison. I don't want any such stupid rumors floated on Wall Street. In the meantime, I'll get some people looking into this immediately."

"Sir, was someone in the Moscow office of Caspian recently killed?" Morrison asked.

"Seems I did hear about a young woman being killed in a traffic accident. Traffic is hell on pedestrians in Moscow," Volkoff answered.

■ ■ ■ ■ ■ ■ ■ ■ ■ ■

Blanchard woke up with a seething anger from his dream to be replaced almost immediately with an awful fear. He rang for the nurse. When she arrived, he asked if his sister was in the hospital. He was informed that she was not.

Ten minutes later, a short balding man in a tweed blazer came to Blanchard's bedside.

"Mister Blanchard, my name is Doctor Frank Edwards. Both Doctor Chang and your sister asked if I would stop in to chat a little with you."

"Are you a shrink?" Blanchard asked, but being somewhat difficult to understand since he could move his jaw only slightly. The words sounded like a bad ventriloquist.

"An unfortunate label, but yes, I am a psychologist. I work a lot with severely injured people and try to help them find a means to move beyond the injury," he said.

"Sorry, Doc. No sale here. Life as I knew it is over. There's no alternatives. Disfigured cripples have no life that's worth a shit."

"Obviously I don't agree since I have seen so many people find an alternative. I would not pretend to convince you with arguments and inspirational cases. What I would like to do is simply talk and perhaps assist your own thoughts in exploring avenues you may not be able to consider easily left to your own understandable depression."

"Doc, not now. I'm not interested," Blanchard said.

"Very well. I'll drop around again. Anything I can do for you right now?" The psychologist asked.

"Yes, there is something. I would ask my sister but she's not here. It's very important. Could you try to reach a Miss Irina Petrenko in Moscow for me? I want to know if she is ok." Blanchard said.

"Sure. She a girl friend?"

"Doc, I just want to know if she is --- all right, that's all. I heard that she might have had an accident. It's important I know right away, that's why I'd rather not wait for my sister," Blanchard said. He told the doctor how to get the number through their website.

Hours later, Dr. Edwards entered the room with Blanchard's sister. The sister looked distressed, not her usual game face to try to bolster her brother's spirits.

"Gordon, this girl, Irina, you never spoke of her to me. Were you close?"

"You might say that. Have you reached her?" Blanchard asked.

Dr. Edwards answered, "I'm afraid she was killed several days ago, Gordon. Struck by a truck while crossing a street in Moscow."

Blanchard made a pitiful groan. "Those assholes killed her. Oh, Christ. Hit and run I bet. Just like me." He was silent for a few moments as tears cascaded down his face from his one eye. "Please, Carol, I need to be alone. I need to go to sleep. Can you get the nurse?"

. . . .

I took the key card from my pocket. It read *Chelsea Hotel, 222 West Twenty-Third Street, New York.* My papers were spread all over the bed. I sat down at the desk and reviewed my report on my laptop.

I concluded that I had pretty compelling evidence against at least senior people at Caspian. No telling how far a full-blown investigation would get into Global Resources & Logistics stateside. GRL stock will tank if Wall

Street were to get wind of what might come down. My own stock holdings and options would suffer, but I didn't care.

The FBI offices in New York City are located at 26 Federal Plaza, just a short ride from Chelsea by subway. I came out at the Chambers Street Station and walked the three blocks to the Federal Building. I gave my name to the receptionist and said that I needed to speak with an agent to report a crime.

After some minutes, a man in his early thirties with a military style haircut came up to me and introduced himself as Special Agent White and led me to his small office. Once seated, he asked me what it was that I wanted to report.

"First of all, I'm a senior internal auditor for Global Resources & Logistics. I assume you're familiar with the name?" I said.

"Of course, Mister Blanchard. Major international corporation. Into energy I believe. Correct?" he said.

"Right, and a host of other enterprises. I'll get right to it, Agent White. I have documentation that implicates senior executives at GRL's subsidiary Caspian Enterprises, based in Russia, with money laundering, bribery, and corruption. I also believe they have killed at least one person that helped me get this evidence."

"I see. That's quite a serious bunch of allegations. Before we continue, would you mind giving me some personal information so that we can verify who you say you are?"

I obliged by showing him my driver's license and passport. He offered me a coffee while he excused himself for a few minutes.

Fifteen minutes later he returned with another man, introducing him as Special Agent MacIntyre.

"Agent MacIntyre is also an accountant so he is better qualified to discuss what you have to tell us, Mister Blanchard."

I told him about my recent project in Moscow. I pulled copies of documents from my briefcase, explaining each one as I went along.

"These are just a few samples. My full report is on this CD. There are extensive addendums which cite contracts, transactions, etc. that support my conclusions."

MacIntyre was absorbed in the documents. White asked, "And the murder you allege? Who was that?"

"Her name was Irina Petrenko. She worked in the IT Department at Caspian. She was assigned to help me with reviewing documents for my audit. She turned out to be clever and somewhat suspicious of her bosses. At any rate, she led me to all sorts of material. After I returned to New York, I learned she was run over in the street in Moscow."

"And why do you think it was murder?"

"It was a hit and run. Plus, I have reason to believe that certain people had learned what I had discovered," I said.

"Do you think you are in danger, Mister Blanchard?" Agent White asked.

That stopped me. In my rage I had not thought about that possibility. Or had I? Why was I hold up in a hotel rather than my apartment. "I'm not sure. But at any rate I'm staying at a hotel rather than my own place."

"Are you going to the office?"

I had not thought about that. "I'm not sure."

"Well, Mister Blanchard, if your allegations are true, it might be helpful if you were on the inside. If you do not return to work, aren't your superiors going to be suspicious?"

"I guess you're right," I said.

"Have you given anyone this report?"

"Not yet. But I told the Company Controller about what I discovered. He's expecting my report before he'll do anything, but I know he called the Chief Operating Officer just after I told him what I had found."

MacIntyre said, "Let's do this, Mister Blanchard. First, we'll get a stenographer and have you give a statement about everything you know. In the meantime, we will get some people to start checking on some of your findings to see if we can validate them. I would like to suggest you start work immediately on creating a somewhat sanitized version of your report. Leave out as much real evidence as you can while still making your allegations to top management credible. The intention is to see if we can buy some time before they start obscuring the audit trail."

I nodded my agreement. "I'd like a favor. I'd like to know what your Russian counterparts say about the death of Irina Petrenko."

"We'll see what we can do, Mister Blanchard."

I left the Federal Building and went back to the Chambers Street subway station to catch the Eighth Avenue Line train. It was rush hour and a fair size crowd built up behind me. I was standing close to the platform edge. I could hear the train approaching. From behind, a man put his hand on my shoulder and spoke to me in an east European language. Russian? He said something to a man next to him who answered in the same dialect. Both grinned as they pushed me off the platform.

· · · · · · · · · ·

A monitor alarm went off. A nurse arrived moments later, followed by the duty resident. Blanchard's heart rate was elevated to over 190 beats per minute. His systolic blood pressure was 170, and respiration was over 50 a minute. His upper body was almost writhing. His face was perspiring profusely, yet he was seemingly still asleep.

"Get me a ---" the doctor started to order the nurse, but saw that the patient had opened his eyes. "Mister Blanchard, are you all right? Are you in pain?"

No I'm not fucking all right. I'm half dead and crippled Blanchard wanted to say but checked himself. "I'm ok. Bad dream is all."

After his vital signs returned to normal, the doctor and nursing staff left. A short time after, his sister entered the room. She kissed his forehead and held his hand.

"The Doctor seemed concerned about your episode. What you just went through. God, I thought something life threatening was going on. They wouldn't let me in until you were stable. What happened, Gordon?"

"I don't know what this medical thing is that you and the Doctor are talking about, but I've got to tell you about my dreams. Carol, I'm having this dream, it's the same dream each time, about my work just prior to my being run down. The damndest thing is that the dream seems like a continuing story. More than that, I'm whole in the dream. I can walk. I can feel it. I have two arms and hands. When I wake up, I return to this. Is this to be my life?"

"Gordon, please talk with Doctor Edwards. I know how you feel about talking to a psychologist, but it can't possibly do any harm. You're the one who always argued for being open and objective. For my sake if not your own, would you please talk to him?"

Blanchard reluctantly agreed and told his sister, perhaps tomorrow.

After some pleasantries, his sister left. Both were finding it difficult to fill their time together with conversation. They had too many differences in perspectives on life, complicated further by his depression.

After a number of hours, the pain returned, subtlety at first, but with a steadily increasing intensity that finally caused him to give into medication. This time he was not sure he wished to enter sleep. The dream was becoming an alternate reality full of its own dangers.

. . . .

Fucking filth. I wasn't hurt by the fall, but the subway track area was a repository for every conceivable kind of trash. Plastic bags, drink containers, wrappers of every sort, and more than one condom. I stood up and heard the sound of the oncoming train.

"Jesus, buddy, take my hand!" a big guy yelled.

I did, and he hoisted me from within seconds of a terrible death as the express came through without stopping at the station.

A small crowd gathered around me, but I shoved through and escaped onto Chambers Street. I realized that I was now a target. I couldn't go back to my hotel, much less the office. Pulling out my wallet I determined I had credit cards and a few twenties. Hailing a cab, I told him to take me to a small hotel on the Upper West Side, not far from Columbia University. I had stayed there years ago for a couple of weeks before getting an apartment when I was going to school.

Once in the hotel room, I called Special Agent White. I told him what had happened, but I must have sounded semi-hysterical.

"Calm down, Mister Blanchard. Are you sure it wasn't just an accident? The crush of people?"

"Absolutely, fucking not. I was pushed. Both hands on my back. Two East European assholes. They spoke to each other. They were Russian, and somebody at Caspian sent them. Maybe even somebody from Global."

"Where are you, Mister Blanchard?"

I hesitated for a few moments, then answered "I'd rather no one knew where I was."

"Mister Blanchard, if there's someone out to kill you, we can protect you."

I would rather keep my hotel a secret so I told him to meet me at a bar I knew of just across the Harlem River in the Bronx. "I'll meet you there in one hour." I hung up before Agent White could argue.

Ten minutes later I left my room and took the elevator to the lobby. There were a couple of guys reading newspapers and a desk clerk talking to a customer at the counter. As I walked past, the customer said something to the clerk. The accent was unmistakably Russian.

Jesus Christ I said to myself and quickly walked through the front door and started to run. Behind me there were shouts. No accented English, just plain Russian. I heard 'дерьмо', meaning 'shit' in Russian. I ran like shit.

It was semi-dark. I was comparatively small compared with the two gorillas chasing me so I was gaining a little distance between us. But it felt like a dream. I could not run as fast as I thought I should and I was getting winded. People on the sidewalk stepped aside with some fear.

I came to an alley and tore down it calculating that the more turns I made the more I would gain on my pursuers. Two guys doing a drug deal were startled and dropped cash and dope. "What the fuck?"

I was soaked in sweat as the alley ended in a 'T'. Left was a chain link fence, right was a truck blocking the entire width of the alley. I dropped to my knees, gasping for air.

■ ■ ■ ■ ■ ■ ■ ■ ■ ■

"Mister Blanchard, wake up. Mister Blanchard."

Blanchard was soaked in sweat. His chest heaved to grasp enough air. The two nurses holding him down eased their holds on him.

"It seems, Mister Blanchard, that you suffer some acute mental anxiety during sleep. So bad, that it takes on some rather severe physical manifestations. At the least, your heart rate and blood pressure go through the roof. With the internal trauma you suffered in the accident, I am genuinely concerned that these episodes could be very dangerous. You're totally soaked in sweat from the level of exertion," Doctor Chang said. "You need to talk to Doctor Edwards. We need to understand what is going on when you go to sleep."

After he was bathed and fed, his sister and Dr. Edwards came into the room.

"Gordon, please tell us what is going on. Doctor Chang is concerned. You're the only family I have, and I love you. Please?" his sister pleaded.

Blanchard debated with Dr. Edwards, but resisted telling him about the dream. Eventually the Doctor ceased trying to persuade him and left the room. His sister stayed.

The torment of his wrecked body while awake and the fear when he dreamed was becoming too much. He wished an end to it all. Death would be fine, but not this protracted agony. If he only had the means he would gladly end his own life.

"I'll tell you what is going on, Carol. And he did for the next twenty minutes.

At the end of his narrative, his sister said, "That's quite a story, Gordon. You've had a number of huge stresses hit you all at once. First this corruption you think you discovered within your corporation, your accident, and then hearing of the loss of this Russian girl that you were apparently fond of. Maybe the dreams are a way of escaping your physical condition and these events."

Blanchard shook his head in denial. "Dream, Carol, not dreams. It's one continuation of the same dream. I go to sleep and live another life, or another reality. Problem is, it's hell there too. It's no goddamn escape," Blanchard said.

"Gordon, Doctor Chang says that during your sleep the last couple of days, your heart rate and respiration are so high that you could literally have heart failure. Doctor Edwards even talked about medication to calm your mind."

"Not yet, Carol. It'll resolve itself soon," Blanchard said.

Some hours later the pain was such that he had to have the morphine. He prepared to face the dream.

■ ■ ■ ■ ■ ■ ■ ■ ■ ■

I got up from the pavement somewhat recovered from the running. Where to go though? The rear of the stake truck blocked the alley with no room to squeeze by the sides. There was commotion behind him.

"What you white motherfuckers doin'?" one of the dopers yelled at the Russians.

"Out of way, assholes," one of the Russians said.

Suddenly, there was a loud report, followed soon by several others. Christ, it was gunfire! I plunged down on my stomach in the filthy alley and crawled under the length of the truck. Once clear I took off running again.

After maybe ten blocks and confident that I had lost my pursuers, I telephoned Agent White. He was still at the bar waiting for me, clearly pissed that I was late.

White had a table in the back of the bar. Even in the low light I looked a mess.

"What the hell happened?" White asked as I walked up to the table.

"A couple of Russians tried to get me. They ran into a couple of New York's finest and I got away."

"The NYPD got them?"

"No. A couple of low-lifes doing a drug deal."

"Clearly we need to get you somewhere safe. I'll call a car here with some help," Agent White said.

"No. I'm not going to sit in some apartment for a year while you guys try to make a case. What I do want to know is what you've found out."

A waitress came by and I ordered a scotch and White ordered another beer. I went to the restroom to wash up and the drinks arrived when I returned.

"Well, Mister Blanchard, we've uncovered enough to expand the investigation. We think that the magnitude of illegal activities is far more pervasive than what you discovered."

"Who are the senior people you think are involved?" I asked.

"At Caspian, almost assuredly Nikolai Melnikov, the managing director. Then there's a senior guy by the name of Konstantin Yudin. And of course there's this Vadim Sorokin that's implicated in your research. Seems things are less sophisticated over there. These guys were pretty crude in some of their transactions. Hardly any attempt at covering them up as legitimate dealings. And you consider that we have to get this through Russian sources and their bungling bureaucracy."

White went on to explain that Melnikov and Yudin had headed two companies that had done business together before being acquired by Global. Melnikov's company owned power plants and refineries. Yudin's was a transportation company. Sorokin was an ex-deputy minister in the government. White added that there was strong circumstantial evidence that Sorokin was connected with Russian organized crime.

In general, Caspian was selling energy, largely to government agencies at above market prices, greasing the deals with heavy kickbacks. On the supply side, they were leasing transportation logistics consisting of shipping, rail, and trucking at below market prices with firms heavily suspected of laundering Asian drug money. The key figure appeared to be Sorokin, seemingly with his broad array of contacts, both governmental and criminal.

"Now the interesting guy is your Mister Volkoff. Executive Vice President and Chief Operating Officer of Global Resources & Logistics. Fortune 500 company and darling of Wall Street." White said. "Volkoff put the Russian acquisitions together. It got him promoted and made him rich."

White continued, "Volkoff has an interesting background. Born in Kiev. Age fifty-nine. Undergraduate degree in economics at the University of Moscow. MBA from Wharton. Worked for a number of large U.S. and European firms. Spent most of his time working deals in many of the former Soviet states. He's close with both Melnikov and Yudin. More than close with Sorokin. Vadim Sorokin is Eric Volkoff's brother-in-law."

"You're saying that if these other Russians are dirty, it's a good bet that Volkoff is part of it too? Maybe even the head guy?" I said.

"Almost has to be. The whole architecture of Caspian is his doing. These are his guys. Besides, Volkoff has a reputation as a real shark. Hard to envision his Russian colleagues going off the reservation without Volkoff's knowledge. Add to that the kind of stuff you uncovered and what we have found, it suggests that somebody high up on this side of the water at Corporate had to know what was going on."

The pattern was clear. I report the findings of my audit to the Controller thinking I'm going to help them contain and correct the abuses. That information makes its way quickly to Volkoff. Volkoff calls Sorokin. Sorokin gets a couple of his 'people' to remove the problem.

"Where does Volkoff live?" I asked.

"Right here in Manhattan," Agent White answered. "And that's even more of a reason to get you somewhere where we can protect you. Our case will be that much stronger with you as an insider witness, and your help with navigating the corporate stuff. I'm afraid I must insist, Mister Blanchard."

"All right, let me go to the toilet first," I said. Instead, I left through the back door of the bar then took off running once again. This time with rage rather than fear.

. . . .

Blanchard woke. He felt somewhat better than the last time. The nurse commented that he was still agitated while he slept, but not so much so that the doctor had to be summoned. That may have been because he had decided not to be the hunted anymore in the dream. The rest of his waking hours that day were spent putting together a plan of action; a plan for the Dream. This was taking an out-of-body experience to a new level.

. . . .

I checked into the Sofitel Hotel on Forty-Fourth Street in Midtown Manhattan. It was early morning. My clothes were still soiled from crawling under the truck. To the desk clerk, my appearance was explained away as resulting from an accident. My luggage would arrive later. 'Whatever', the clerk's expression implied. As long as the credit card was valid and the driver's license matched. I asked the clerk for a recommendation for a men's clothing store close by. The clerk also provided a set of basic toiletries. At the small hotel store, I bought a clean shirt and chinos and returned to my room to cleanup.

The haberdashery was only a short walk. "Good morning, Sir. Can I help you?"

"I hope so. I need a suit, shirt, tie, shoes, the works. The damn airlines lost my luggage and I have an important meeting in a few hours. Do you have a tailor that can do the alterations right away?" I asked.

"Well, I'll have to see. We usually need at least twenty-four hours."

"There's a couple of hundred in a tip if you can manage it. I'm a perfect forty regular so it's just the trousers that will need alteration."

"In that case, I'm sure we can accommodate you, Sir. What color were you looking for?"

Thirty minutes later I left with a promise of having the suit ready in two hours. My next stop was a luggage retailer where I picked up a brief case. After that, I took the subway some distance to a less affluent part of town for my final purchase.

A buzzer sounded as I entered. "What can I do for you?" the clerk in the gun shop said.

"I'm looking for a pellet gun. You know, a CO_2 gun. A handgun. It's for my son's birthday.

The shopkeeper showed me several. I chose what appeared as a full size authentic looking 9mm automatic. "I'll take it. And I'll need a shoulder holster too. A real one just like detectives wear."

As the clerk boxed up my purchases and ran my credit card, he admonished me, "Mind you tell your son to be careful with this. It's not something he should fool around with. Even up close you can't tell it from a real 9mm. Even has the heft. Point this at a cop and he'll blow you away."

Odd. It seemed like I just left the gun shop, yet I was dressed in my new suit, crisp shirt, and new shoes. I had no recollection of picking up the clothes at the haberdashery. An expensive briefcase was at my feet at the outdoor coffee shop I knew well. It was directly across from the corporate offices of Global Resources & Logistics.

My watch said it was five-thirty. I saw the black limousine pull up across the street. I placed a ten-dollar bill under my coffee cup and walked to a position on the sidewalk slightly behind the limo.

The limo driver stood adjacent to the rear door waiting for Eric Volkoff.

Volkoff appeared moments later. The driver opened the door. He was a big guy, barrel-chested with a too-tight black jacket. Volkoff was smaller by a hundred pounds and elegantly dressed.

I made my move by stepping between Volkoff and the open door. The driver was on the other side of Volkoff. I stopped Volkoff with the faux 9mm in his abdomen.

"What the hell ---" Volkoff said.

"Do anything to make a scene and I'll kill you," I said.

The driver, and apparently a bodyguard, pulled a weapon from a shoulder holster. He looked vaguely familiar.

"Tell your man to give me his gun right now or I'll kill you," I said.

Volkoff hesitated and just stared at me. "I don't care if I die. Do you, Mister Volkoff?" I said.

Volkoff said something in Russian to his man. The bodyguard handed over his weapon. We all got into the limousine. I ordered him to drive to Volkoff's residence on Park Avenue. To Volkoff's questions, I told him to shut up.

The limousine was parked in the underground garage and all three of us made our way to the top floor to Volkoff's penthouse. We went to the study where Volkoff had an impressive array of computers and monitors. I ordered Volkoff into a chair in front of a computer. The bodyguard was ordered to sit on the floor in a corner.

"Know who I am, Mister Volkoff?"

"No."

"I'm Gordon Blanchard. You may have heard my name."

Volkoff could not totally hide his surprise. "From Global?" he said. "What the hell are you doing?'

"I'm here to have you tell me what's been going on."

Volkoff paused a few moments before answering. "I was told you had some sensitive information after you returned from Russia. Then you went missing. We have been trying to locate you to get your report. I'm told that you have made serious accusations that must be investigated immediately."

"I've been out of contact because you have been trying to have me killed."

"That's ridiculous, Blanchard," Volkoff said. "We don't have people killed."

I spent the next few minutes bringing Volkoff up to speed on recent events; attempts on my life, discussions with the FBI; the murder of Irina.

"Blanchard, that's absurd. Nobody at Global would engage in that sort of violence," Volkoff said.

"Bullshit. Nobody would do anything without your blessing, Volkoff. But I'm not going to argue with you. What you're going to do is type out a full confession on the computer. All the illegal actions at Caspian. The names. The murder of Irina Petrenko."

"There's no way that I'll do that, Blanchard," Volkoff said.

"If you don't I'll shoot you. Maybe in the leg first, but I will shoot you. You will not live unless I get that confession. Now do it!"

"You're a virgin, Blanchard. Caspian is the way international business is conducted. You don't make money in places like the former Soviet Union like you would in the United States. You've got to deal with the reality of the environment."

"That just makes you another corporate asshole. But you're also a murderer. What I want to know first is about killing people. Specifically Irina Petrenko."

Volkoff reluctantly turned to the computer but did not start typing.

"I'll help you, Volkoff. Start with why Irina Petrenko was murdered." Then I jammed the barrel of the gun hard into the back of his head. Volkoff still did not start typing. I then moved back slightly and shot Volkoff in the toes of his right foot.

"Goddamn!" Volkoff screamed.

"Tell me that you ordered her killing, Volkoff," I said. "And mine also."

Volkoff took several moments to gather himself with the terrible pain from his damaged foot. "All right, all right!" He was sweating profusely. "I didn't order her killed. That would have been Sorokin."

"But you gave the instructions. Let me guess; something like 'take care of the problem'. Correct?" I hit Volkoff in the head with the barrel of my gun.

Volkoff grunted from the blow. I had his attention now. "Listen, Blanchard. I told Sorokin to contain the problem. I didn't tell him to kill anyone."

The bodyguard stirred and I pointed the gun on him. Volkoff then bolted out of his chair and grabbed for my gun. I shot him in the chest, but was still knocked down by his charge.

Pushing Volkoff's body off me, I was faced with the now standing bodyguard yelling at me in Russian. He was pointing a gun at me. Each of us shot repeatedly.

■ ■ ■ ■ ■ ■ ■ ■ ■ ■

"Gordon, how are you feeling today?" his sister said. She was sitting at his bedside as he woke.

"Ok. Actually, better I guess." the remains of the dream still lingered. He felt some satisfaction. Some sense of revenge realized, if only in the form of a dream.

His sister made some small talk, before showing him a newspaper. "I thought you'd want to know that the *Times* reported a senior executive at Global was murdered in New York."

"What? Who?"

"His name was Eric Volkoff. Did you know him?"

"Know him? Of course. What happened?" I asked.

"The paper says he was murdered in his penthouse apartment, along with his chauffeur. He was apparently Russian. Is he involved in what you discovered wrong when you were in Moscow, Gordon?"

"Probably. What else does the newspaper say?"

"They don't have any suspects, investigation continues, etc, etc. Then there's something about a possible Justice Department investigation of Global, but there's no confirmation. Unnamed sources sort of thing."

Blanchard absorbed the information with a sense of disorientation. How could the dream have paralleled reality? He couldn't have known about the actual event to have integrated it into his dream.

"Gordon, the Doctor says you could try getting into a wheel chair tomorrow. It would do you good. It's time you thought about ---about---"

Blanchard interrupted with, "About getting on with my life? Carol, it ended with the accident. We've been through this over and over. Some things can never get better."

They argued for a while. Carol cried and said she could not continue like this. She left frustrated and angry. Blanchard felt sorry for his sister, and for himself. The only thing at the moment was going to sleep again and revisiting the dream.

• • • • • • • • •

"Hey, bro, you awake?" a black man missing a couple of teeth said.

I was in a bed and this guy was in an adjacent bed. It was a large room with other beds and people. It was a hospital ward.

"Where am I?" I asked.

"You're in Belleview, motherfucker. The police ward. Fucked up bad from what the doctors were sayin'. What'd you do to get yourself in here? Cops shoot you?"

"Don't know," I said, but I remembered shooting Volkoff and shooting the big Russian bodyguard. I tried to raise up on my arms. My gown fell off revealing heavy bandages on my abdomen. My legs wouldn't move.

"Hey, Jack, you ain't goin' anywhere, you're fucking crippled. Heard the Doc say you were shot in the spine. You can't walk and he wasn't sure if you could even shit right," the man said, then convulsed in laughter.

"No! No! ----- No!"

• • • • • • • • •

"Code Blue, stat! Room three-one-five!" the nurse yelled into an intercom. She ripped open Gordon Blanch-ard's gown and applied a stethoscope to his chest. The heart monitor flat-lined. A team arrived with the crash cart of cardiac emergency equipment.

CPR and repeated electro-shock applications from a defibrillator failed to revive Gordon Blanchard's heart.

THE END

By Douglas Clark

"Vengeance is in my heart, death in my hand,
blood and revenge are hammering in my head."
William Shakespeare, Titus Andronicus II.iii

"Carlos, come on, try to tell us what you do without violating your oath to national security," the girlfriend of my best friend said. She had had a fair amount to drink, as had everyone at our apartment.

"Listen, I just work with the computer systems. I don't see any of the interesting stuff. There's no glamour. It's no different than your jobs," I said.

That was not true. I saw all sorts of highly sensitive material. My job was to design information extraction programs for various National Security Agency databases and other government security sources such as the Central Intelligence Agency and the Defense Intelligence Agency. Creating the functional algorithms for such software programs gave me not only access to highly sensitive information, but also an understanding of how the information was organized. Even reading excerpts was exciting. This was stuff that only a select few saw. It had taken several years to obtain the highest security clearance possible.

Our friends were all young and all worked for the government, but all of them in non-sensitive roles with such agencies as the General Accounting Office or the Department of the Interior. One was a congressional staffer. Angela my girlfriend was the only other one of the group aside from me with a security clearance since she worked for the Justice Department.

"Bullshit, you're a computer geek-spook, Carlos. We're only fucking bureaucrats, but you're on the edge of all those dark secrets. Give us average citizens something, Carlos. Some little tidbit of something tantalizing. No national secrets. Perhaps something of a sexual nature, "a twenty-something young man said, raising a round of laughter.

"Come on boys and girls, leave Carlos alone," Angela said as she carried a glass and a new bottle of wine to her guests. "I've tried all means of sexual persuasion and he still won't talk. Not likely he'll tell you Neanderthals anything."

"And believe me, Angela can be most persuasive," I said, grabbing her waist and kissing her, almost spilling her wine.

A somewhat plump young woman said good-naturedly, "I don't want to hear about your sexual escapades. It is truly unfair that you Latins are culturally and socially compelled to screw with an abandon and passion not inclined to the rest of the world." Her husband raised his eyebrows and went back to his beer.

My parents are from Guatemala, but I was born in the U.S. Angela is third generation Italian. We both have somewhat dark complexions with dark hair. We are both the same height, which makes Angela tall. Her legs and hair are longer than mine, though. She's a beauty, I'm average. We're both Latin I guess in the broadest definition.

I met Angela in graduate school. We both have master's degrees in information technology. I'm a systems engineer; she's a software engineer. We're both bright. Bright enough to lead us on a harrowing journey of disillusionment. Not with each other, but with the government's power as we came to know it. We've been living together for three years. After what we went through over the last sixteen months, this has made us closer than ever, but cynical to the point of paranoia.

Our lives changed one Sunday afternoon. I was reading the newspaper having coffee when my mother called from California.

"Hi, Mom. Kind of early out there. Everything OK?"

"No, Carlos, it's not."

"Father?"

"No, your father's fine. It's your Tio Ramon. He was kidnapped."

"Jesus, what do'ya mean kidnapped?"

"Carlos, they want money. Money for Ramon's return."

"You mean they've demanded a ransom? Tio Ramon's not wealthy. Why?"

"That's all we know. Four men with hoods broke into their house just after midnight. They hurt your Tia Esperanza, but she'll be all right. She got a call a couple of hours ago demanding a ransom of 500,000 dollars."

"They don't have that kind of money. Neither do you and Dad. The police – what do they say?"

"Carlos, we don't know very much. Esperanza is so upset I can't really get much information. Your Father and I are leaving for Guatemala City on the next flight. I'll call you when we get there and I know more."

My mother's brother was a prominent professor of economics in Guatemala. A former cabinet minister turned opposition party advocate. He had tried to counter the entrenched corruption only to be forced to resign.

Ramon Valverdez did not leave public life with his removal from the government. The President had in fact made a terrible blunder. My Uncle was a Harvard alumnus with a large network of contacts throughout South America, Mexico, and the United States. Without any constraints of office, he viscously attacked the government and particularly the military. His credentials and contacts brought unwanted bad press to Guatemala, particularly in Washington.

Almost a week after hearing of my uncle's kidnapping, my father called. "Carlos --- the worst has happened. Ramon has been murdered." For several moments both my father and I wept.

Finding his composure, my father said, "His body was found in a park. He'd been shot in the head. Executed."

"Mother? How is she?" I asked.

"She's managing. She's been trying to help your Tia Esperanza. Unfortunately, Esperanza is not managing well."

"There's something else, Carlos," my father continued. "I have been doing some checking. I am convinced that your uncle was killed by the Military. This business of a kidnapping for ransom does not seem to stand up."

Several weeks later my father called again. "Listen, Son, I am certain that Ramon was murdered by the Military, maybe by orders from the President himself. I've had two threats on my own life. Your Mother is already on her way back home. I'm even calling you from a public phone in case they have listening devices at your uncle's home."

"Jesus, Dad, get out of Guatemala now! You've got no power down there and no protection." I was suddenly uneasy about his safety. In all my trips to Guatemala it was sunny and friendly. Now it felt like the portrayal in the history books of its dictators and death squads.

"I'm a U.S. citizen with some influence. I don't think they would dare risk an incident with the United States by detaining or harming me. Worst that can happen is they'll deport me."

He was wrong. Two days later, a bomb was thrown into a café killing my father and three others, injuring several more.

My grief was abject. I did not realize the depth of my love until he was gone. Angela too. She was the daughter he never had and she adored him.

My father's body was returned to the States for burial. My mother was virtually bedridden under sedation. As for me, the depth of my own depression surprised me. I loved my father of course, but we never seemed to be as close as I thought we should be. He was kind and always interested in me, yet he was often remote and introspective.

Only with Angela's care was I able to get through those initial days of grieving.

After a couple of weeks I began moving beyond the grief. Now I wanted to retaliate. I did not have names, but I knew them collectively. They were beyond any laws. That's when I decided to do something constructive, or I should say, destructive in order to have my revenge. If information was power, I had at my grasp an enormous potential with the vast databases of the NSA, CIA, and Defense. The question was if I was sufficiently clever to get anything useful and not get caught. More than that, if I did find anything, how could I use it to destroy those that had killed my father and uncle?

I would not be hacking in the truest sense of the definition. What I would be doing was risking career and jail for violating all sorts of federal laws. I already had access to at least enter most secured government databases as part of my responsibilities. The task would be to cover my tracks. Software security was not my principle expertise so I would need help there. Once into the system, I knew my way around better than anyone.

"Angela. I need your help with something, if you're willing." Software security was very much her area of expertise.

"Of course. What do you mean, if I'm willing?"

"I want to get to those that killed my father and uncle. Bring 'em down. All the way. Get them killed if I can."

"Whoa, Carlos -- what are you talking about?"

"These guys are in databases. Databases I have access to. Those I don't, like banks, can be hacked into."

"Carlos, that isn't smart. You'll get caught. We'll get caught. Federal laws carry stiff sentences. Besides, even if you get secret information, how can you use it? You can't take it to the media. They'll want to know the source. They'll want to independently corroborate."

"I know all that, Angela. I haven't thought it through yet. But I will find a way to use the information once I get my hands on it."

"Christ, that's not much of a plan to risk everything on."

"Damn it, what would you have me do, nothing?" I was frustrated and angry and taking it out on Angela. "These fuckers'll get away with these murders just like all the other killings down there. I have to do something, Angela. I need it. I need it for me."

She came to where I was sitting and brought my head close to her body.

"I'll help you because I love you. I know you. You'll try it without me. I don't intend for us to get caught, so I'll help."

"I love you, Angela." And I truly did. We kissed and said nothing for several minutes.

"So where do we start?" Angela asked. Emotions put away, she now saw this purely as a technical problem.

"Listen, I'm going to be cautious, I promise. Unless I can find some way to use the information, I won't go very far. I don't want to get caught.

"I assumed you'd be cautious, so where are you going to start?" she responded.

"I have to identify the players first. NSA has broad-based stuff, but the CIA has the real detail. The CIA's intelligence comes from human sources. The NSA's comes mostly from communications intercepts. The United States and Guatemala go way back. The CIA has extensive information on all senior military and government officials in all of Central America. More than that, they have the dirt, or at least what they think is the dirt on these guys. Special bad habits, weaknesses, suspicions, allegations."

A vague outline of a plan was forming.

"Ok. So you find out who likes to dress up as a woman, who likes young boys. You can't expect to find out who gave the orders to have your father and uncle murdered," Angela argued.

She was obviously correct. And the clarity of my plan suddenly struck me.

"You're right of course, Angela. However, my objective is to destroy the Military. I want more than to just put sand into their machinery. I want them turned into pariahs.

"Even those not guilty?"

"No different than a war, Angela. If they're military, they're legitimate targets. I want to retaliate against the institution. Besides, the Guatemalan Military has been a murderous bunch of assholes for decades."

"Sounds like a rationalization to me. We'll see how it plays out, if you get that far. I'm telling you, if it morally bothers me, I'll fight you on it, Carlos."

One might think that extracting computer information would be a cup of tea since it was my job to design the search programs I would be looking at. The problem however was not accessing the information, but leaving no traces of my unauthorized activity. You see, all computer systems track every activity and the user's identity. Therefore, I couldn't leave a trail of electronic fingerprints searching databases for Guatemalan Military officers. A little obvious even for sloppy computer security.

Another thought struck me as I was plotting with Angela to become a computer ninja. How would I get the information out of the building? The answer was simple, I probably wouldn't. So that would mean long hours. It would also mean finding a way to securely store my collected files.

I was starting to think the problems were insurmountable. If it were not for Angela, I would not have even gotten started. For the next several weeks, Angela gave me an advanced course in systems security. Since she did not have access to our system it was like a pilot talking to a novice trying to land an aircraft. She would give me my tasks each day, and I would dutifully report back. We would work for hours, Angela mostly, writing code that I would use on the NSA system.

"This is a real bitch. I don't see how we're going to get over this last hurdle. We've been working on it for a week."

"Come on, Carlos. Here, have some more pizza."

"I'll take the wine instead."

"Let me show you something I've been thinking about. I haven't got it totally worked out, but here's the main idea," Angela said. She had been scribbling on a notepad.

"We get you in as a super-user just as we discussed with a Trojan horse program. From that position we can scan all running jobs. We'll write a program that allows you to identify databases, individual files, or systems and individual computers of interest. The program identifies users currently logged-in and accessing your areas of interest. The key is to intercept their log-out. At this point, they're off, or think they're off, and you then piggyback to run your queries. You log-out when finished as the original user session. The real user never sees his on-line time anyway. If they did, they wouldn't recognize the extra time. No reason for Systems Admin to question." Angela paused. "What do think?"

"What if the real user logs back in while I'm still in the session?"

"Just another log-in. No reason you can't log-in simultaneously multiple times."

"What about the IP address identification?"

"Easy to write the program to maintain the same IP address of the original, legitimate log-in user."

"Ok, I see what you mean. But the Trojan horse? What ideas do you have there?"

"I'm sure I can get our program inserted. After all, you're already a highly accessed user. You've already got me the fundamentals on the NSA's computer security. The problem is we can't use your access capabilities because it traces back to you. That means we have to design an elegant entry and exit method that does not use your identification. And because you can't leave the program in the system, you'll have to re-install it every time. If I can come up with more than one entry method that's even better since it further confuses any pattern," she said.

"How the hell do we test all this?" I asked.

"I'll try it on a couple of our systems at Justice. Anything I try I can pass off as anti-hacking experimentation."

"By the way, this is how you get the data out," she said and tossed me a package of small CDs the size of credit cards of the type used in marketing promotions.

It took two more weeks for Angela to write the program and another week to test it on the Justice Department systems.

"It works, Carlos. I got the program installed and identified my area of interest. There were several users logged-in each time I tried it. I actually piggybacked on two users at the same time. Copied some data. Logged off and the program de-installed. I went back and checked the activity report. The two users indicated a single session each, only longer than their actual time. There was no trace of the program. No record identifying me as even accessing the system during the time I was searching the database. No tracks at all!"

Angela sat on my lap and kissed me. "Am I brilliant or what, Honey?"

"You do write elegant code. Not bad looking either for all those brains."

"Let's go do things, sailor," she said as she pulled me to the bedroom.

We celebrated with lovemaking, cooked a couple of steaks, and got a little drunk. It was a Friday night. No more working this weekend. Monday would be my first go at the NSA systems.

My first task was to identify the ranking Guatemalan Military officers and map out the organizational structure. I installed the Trojan horse program and waited for the signal that another user had accessed the database I was interested in. As he logged-out, I stayed on in his place. I worked for about an hour before logging off. The product of my initial search was downloaded onto a mini-CD, which I subsequently placed behind a credit card in my wallet.

I was physically sweating as I left the building that evening.

"Well show me what you got," Angela burst out as I got home. I had called her on my cell phone to tell her I was all right.

"Jesus. I thought security would be suspicious for sure," I said as I inserted the CD into my desktop computer.

Both of us scanned down through the listing of military officers from the middle-level ranks to the top. "Know what any of these acronyms mean?" Angela asked.

"No, but that will be easy enough. Besides, I'm going to focus on their Internal Security Forces and the few top officers. The Internal Security Forces are like their secret police. No civilian oversight. Typical banana republic shit."

After several days, I had not only identified senior officers of the internal security force, but had scanned through a wealth of intelligence reports from the CIA concerning backgrounds and associations of these officers. Using a search engine, I identified keywords and phrases appearing in these reports to identify a shorter list. Words like 'killing',' torture', 'suspected' produced a special list.

"How much of this is true?" Angela asked.

"Probably a lot of it, at least some. CIA fucks up a lot, but then it's usually when they try to do something with the intel."

"Like us trying to do something?" She asked. I just gave her a glance and returned to the computer monitor.

"Like this Captain Herrera," *Reputed to have killed several prostitutes. Torture confirmed in two known cases. Source: Operative codename Felix. Independently confirmed through prison inmates as relayed to Father Timothy Callvares as told to --------.*"

"Another report: *Captain Herrera led squad of Internal Security Forces that murdered five members of the Reyes family. Miguel Reyes was a newspaper reporter critical of the government and probable member of the P.F.G.*

Unconfirmed reports suggest the rape of the two teenaged Reyes girls. Source: Operative code name Felix through bribing of medical personnel."

"Sounds like Felix gets around."

"Yeah, his name shows up a few more times with reports on other military officers."

We worked well into the early morning mapping out the key officers of the Military's Internal Security Forces. We had enough to develop a target list of officers potentially guilty of supervising torture and murder. It was not quite like the death squads of El Salvador several decades ago, but the Guatemalan Military was still exercising a power through selective intimidation. After all, Guatemala had invented the concept of government sponsored death squads and exported it to El Salvador.

Where to hide the CD? Major obstacle. If we were ever discovered, we did not want this found as evidence. Angela came up with a brilliant solution.

"I love it. Christ, I'd make a hell of a spy," she said. "We need to update the data on the CD daily and move it back and forth. Right?"

"Of course," I answered. Feeling a little stupid by not seeing where she was going.

"It's small. You carry it in your wallet. Why? Because you have some porn videos on it. Wouldn't want such a thing found in your desk." Angela said warming to explaining the solution. "What we do is password protect it, but with a subtle wrinkle. Mask the files of the actual data with icons and file extensions that look like video files. I then write a program that booby-traps the actual data files if a certain password is attempted and totally deletes them. That password actually allows you to access real porn videos. Anybody looking over your shoulder should be convinced. You now carry only two CDs, one to download raw data, one to work on. No other files at work or at home. Agreed?"

I smiled broadly. "Agreed. Shit! That's it. It's great!"

"Better yet," she added. "We'll make the porn videos ourselves. More reason not to leave it around since it would embarrass us."

We did not make a digital video that night, but we did practice.

Our database expanded over the next several weeks until we not only had identified suspicious officers but also had assembled fairly expansive profiles. We developed a sense of their individual character and their connections. Some were downright scary if some of the intelligence reports were to be believed.

One evening Angela asked, "We've put together some interesting stuff, Honey, but have you thought what we're going to do with it?"

"Maybe. I've been doing some other probing. Don't know if it will go anyplace, but I've turned up some interesting ideas."

"Like what?"

"Enemies. Enemies to the Guatemalan Military, to the current Government. CIA and NSA have just as much intelligence on opposition people as they do on the Military's thugs. Probably more. Shit, you can even see anticommunist paranoia slip into some reports. Cold War isn't over to the spooks. Anybody vaguely left-of-center is cause for scrutiny."

"So what's the plan?"

"Haven't figured it all out yet, but I think the best way to get to the internal security guys is through their enemies. I can be a conduit to feed them intelligence. I don't know what kind of influence they have, but it'll be a start. At the least, some of these bastards are in for some unpleasant surprises."

"Kind of wish we could do more than just feed stuff to their enemies," Angela commented.

I smiled with a smug expression. "Maybe we can do more. That's the other part of what I discovered. It's two banks. The CIA uses one bank to channel payments to certain military and government types, the other to support informants and even some government opposition. Like a corporation contributing to both political parties. I also discovered the contact person at both banks. The CIA moves money into a dummy account. The internal contact moves monies into the accounts of certain individuals, presumably as instructed from Langley. Langley also knows where the top guys have squirreled away money in secure Caribbean banks."

"Whoa. That's some heavy stuff, Carlos. The CIA would be highly pissed off if you tinker with that."

"Well I don't know exactly how I'd use it yet, but it's got to have big possibilities. It's like secretly watching these assholes have sex."

"So far we haven't done anything we can't back away from, Carlos. Our next step is probably a point of no return."

"I know. And it's me, not *we*, at least legally, Angela. If anything goes wrong, they can't really implicate you if we're careful. And that's the way it'll be. I will not endanger you, Angela."

She heard me and gave me a resigned smile. I had to do this and I wanted to protect her as much as possible. She understood.

"So who are these people that might help?" Angela asked.

"Quite a few actually, but here's the best ones I've come up with. First, a banker. Get this; he's the president of the bank that disperses the CIA money. Knows nothing of the CIA plant who's one of his senior managers."

"There's a newspaper editor. Real pain in the ass to the government. They'd probably kill him if it weren't for his bodyguards. An editorial everyday against the government. Also has strong contacts in the U.S. papers."

Continuing from my notes, "A colonel named Melendez. Hard to figure how he has stayed where he is. They've posted him to some out-of-the-way command. Reports say he is from a wealthy family. Family supported the government in the bad old days too. Reports hint at a strong following among junior officers."

"And lastly, there's Senator Campbell. Senior senator from Pennsylvania. Ranking member of the Foreign Relations Committee."

"You mean a U.S. senator is the subject of CIA intelligence reports?"

"Not exactly the subject," I answered, "but it looks like people opposing the current Guatemalan government have access to his staffers. He's also a big CIA critic."

"So where do we go from here?" Angela asked.

"Now we create trouble."

How that was to happen, I had not yet worked out, but we had all sorts of elements to construct major mischief. We worked on ideas like kids planning pranks. In the details, I sometimes lost sight of why I was doing this. These would be no pranks. I was risking much. I meant to inflict serious harm.

I stepped off the cliff of no return one evening. Angela watched as we electronically took our first step at retaliation. And that's what it was. I was not looking for some concept of justice. It could not mitigate my loss. But it did serve something fundamentally personal. Moving against these murderers gave me a feeling of value. The world cannot be just a place full of evil without some balance created to counter that evil. I was intent on weighing in my share.

I wondered if that was the rationalization every terrorist adopted.

That first step was an e-mail to Hector Benevides, editor of Guatemala City daily newspaper, antagonistic to the current government. I composed it in Spanish.

'Senior Benevides: You do not know me but we are on the same side. That side is against the current government and its secret police. I have lost family and I will have my revenge on those responsible. I have certain resources at my disposal. As a gesture, I have attached a full roster of all military personnel designated as internal security. You can verify by those you know and some investigation of others. I have also attached some compromising photos of one Colonel Torres who is known to you. Advise your interest in further materials and what can be done to damage the enemy. Do not be concerned about security on my end. My e-mail address is a fiction and relegated to a one-time use. Each time I contact you, that address is good only for that one return message. Reply with your level of interest for future contact.'

A roster of all three hundred forty-eight members of the Internal Security Forces of the Republic of Guatemala was enclosed along with three photographs of Colonel Antonio Torres having oral sex administered by what appeared to be a boy about ten years old.

Two hours later a reply came from Benevides, '*Your information was interesting, but holds nothing of value. Photos can be altered in this digital world. How do I know you are who you say, not a spy for the Military?*'

I replied, another one of Angela's program masking my e-mail identification and routing through a succession of Internet servers. '*You don't. But what's the risk? You publish anti-military, anti-government material every day. You be the judge of the material. If you are not interested I can send elsewhere. Advise.*'

It remained to be seen whether Benevides would be of use. As for the photos of Colonel Torres, I e-mailed them to a Mexico City tabloid. They would certainly publish. The tabloid also circulated in Guatemala.

Next there was Captain Flores and Captain Mendez. Flores was having an affair with Mendez' wife according to the prolific CIA informer, Felix. I mailed a letter to Mendez claiming to be another cuckold victim of Flores.

Amazing what mischief can be created when you knew so many secrets. But it was time to get down to some serious actions. The first was against a Sergeant Sandoval. He appeared prominent in the Reyes family atrocities. Other cross-referenced reports implicated him in other incidents of rape and torture.

This would be my first attempt at manipulating the CIA's banking arrangement. With Angela's help, I hacked into a particularly secure area of CIA files. Banks, accounts, and password security to issue disbursement instructions. Hell of a read, but I was only focused on the Guatemalan connections. As for the good sergeant, I instructed the local "paymaster" to deposit $2200 with eleven false deposit records, one per week for the last eleven weeks. False deposit receipts and false cancelled checks drawn on a Mexico City Bank account were to be established. The account could be traced to a Guatemalan anti-government expatriate organization.

"Now what are you going to do?" Angela asked.

"I'm going to get a message to Sandoval's command-ing officer, Captain Herrera. I'll use a message from the CIA's boy Felix to get Herrera the word."

Angela turned quiet and walked away into the kitchen. I followed.

"You knew I intended to do this, Angela."

"And what do you expect will happen?"

"Sandoval will have some explaining to do. And he won't be able to."

"Yeah, and they'll probably kill him. Maybe after they torture him. Is that what you want?"

"How else do I fight them? I told you I was going to wage war. And why should we care about a piece of shit like Sandoval?"

"So you judge him guilty because of some CIA re-ports. Is that enough to have him killed? This is too ugly, Carlos. I'm not going to help anymore. I can't do this," Angela said with tears running down her cheek and stormed into the bedroom.

Fuck. I couldn't argue but I also couldn't stop. I did not tell Angela about another bit of information I had. It concerned an opposition political organization rumored to have committed attacks on military personnel. The ever-present Felix had submitted a report relaying a ru-mor that two lower level security soldiers had been mur-dered, possibly by some vague group supposedly made up of relatives of victims.

Unlike Felix, I had access to other CIA intelligence. It took some digging but I turned up information submit-ted through their embassy based station chief. The group was not vague. The CIA knew one of their leaders to be a local lawyer. The Internal Security Forces had killed his brother.

Any lawyer anywhere in the world today needs ac-cess to the Internet. It was not difficult to get Senior

Villalobos' e-mail address. He must have fallen off his chair when he read my e-mail:

'You do not know me, but I have also shared the loss of a family member murdered by the Military Internal Security Forces. I have access to certain information. The e-mail address above is fictitious, but a reply will reach me. The United States Central Intelligence Agency knows about you as you can see by the attached file. I do not believe they have shared this information with the Guatemalan government. But they do know of you. That is how they work. Information is power. The other file is maybe more interesting. It is a list of all Military Internal Security Forces from the top to the lowest, included with their addresses. There is no way I can convince you that I am on your side. I suggest you watch yourself and check out some of the addresses of where your enemies live. Good luck. Good hunting.'

I asked Angela if she wanted to read it. Still a little upset from a couple of days ago, but couldn't resist.

"Good hunting? Who is this guy?"

"The leader, a leader of some counter-organization to the Military's secret police."

"*Counter*, like in they shoot back?"

"Something like that. Intelligence reports link the group to the killing of a couple security police guys."

"Jesus, Carlos. Do you know what you're doing?"

"Yeah, I do. I'll start a fucking war down there if I have to."

"Honey, I know how you feel. But this kind of getting even....stirring-up the pot and setting some distant people against each other. You don't have any idea what will happen."

"I hope that somebody will start killing these bastards," I responded angrily. "I told you what I'm about. I'm not playing a game. I'm not looking to simply throw sand in their machinery. I want to destroy them."

"Them? And who's 'them'?"

"The Government, the Military, and particularly the Military Internal Security Forces, the fucking secret police, paramilitary units, whatever they're called." I answered.

I was determined now and bent on my course of action. "I'm going to do this, Angela. I mean to inflict real damage on them for what they have done. I'm past any intellectual moralizing bullshit."

Angela just sat still for several moments before saying, "I don't like this, but I understand that you must do this. Just understand I'm having some problems too."

She came to me. We hugged and tears ran down both our cheeks. After several moments, Angela asked, "Are you going to send the e-mail?"

I clicked 'Send'. It felt a little like I had taken a shot at one of them. It was scary. It was also satisfying. I had done something real, something direct. These people had killed some of the secret police. I had just given them the addresses of every one of their enemies. Someone would likely die as a result.

After this initial flurry of action, I ran out of inventive ideas. I avoided invading CIA files for three weeks, using the time instead to plan new tactics. I did pass on some of the same intelligence I gave to the lawyer Villalobos to Senator Campbell. The e-mail was disguised as coming from Villalobos.

I laid out my new ideas to Angela. "So far I've just thrown out damaging information hoping someone would act against these guys."

"Act against? Sounds like government double-speak. Kill them you mean?"

"Yeah, kill them. I've got no problem with that," I retorted.

"Ok, Ok. It just bothers me. Makes me feel dirty. I'm still helping you so don't worry. I just have to say how I feel," she said.

"I know, Honey. And I love you." We hugged and kissed.

"Tomorrow I'm going back in," meaning I was going to see if there were any reports that might suggest any effects of my earlier efforts, and then I would embark on a new tact.

Thanks to the ubiquitous CIA operative, Felix, there was indeed news of my prior mischief. One report indicated the resignation of Colonel Torres following tabloid publication of photos of his deviant sexual exploits. A subsequent report suggested the Colonel's suicide may have been 'assisted'. Felix also reported on the arrest of Captain Mendez, apparently for the murder of a fellow officer. There were no other details but the victim was identified as a Captain Flores. Tough place to mess around with another man's wife. I wondered, not without some guilt, what had happened to the wife.

As to Sergeant Sandoval' fate I never heard. I could only speculate, but it was good odds that he met an ugly end after his commanding officer discovered his bank account and the origin of the deposits.

I knew I should feel some guilt, but I had never seen these people so I could make them into monsters. It was less personal, like dropping bombs from twenty-thousand feet.

The results were encouraging. So encouraging, I wanted something on a broader scale. It took several weeks to devise what I thought to be an elegant manipulation of the bad guys that could bring a lot of them down. The bad guys also included the CIA since they were supporting these thugs. There was a mix of rage and guilt since I worked in the U.S. Intelligence Community.

Not surprising, the CIA was an important conduit of support to the Military of Guatemala. The civilian government served at the pleasure of the Military and current policy in Washington. Nothing new here. The U.S. seemed to always support any government that was in control and friendly to the U.S. Nothing else has ever been the criterion, regardless of the administration. The CIA's record in Latin America for the past fifty years sickened me. I love the United States but not its imperialistic control of its third world southern neighbors.

After an hour of my political and emotional diatribe, I explained my plan to Angela. "The concept is to set all the players against each other using disinformation."

"Who are the players?" Angela asked.

"The Military leadership, the Military's internal security police, the Government, and our own beloved CIA, who of course are acting on behalf of whatever administration is in the White House."

"Don't forget, Carlos, your grudge is with the people that killed your father and uncle, not the U.S. Government. Is it?"

"If I cause damage down there, particularly with the secret police, that's my objective. And I don't give a shit about the U.S. Government's problems that result from my getting to these people. Down there, they're in bed with these assholes."

"Ok, so how do you orchestrate this grand and devious plan?"

"Are you being sarcastic, Angela? Are you with me on this or just going to criticize?"

Angela took my hand. "I'm supporting you, Carlos, but I'm still scared shitless. Our lives have not been the same since your father's death. This revenge is all you think about. We can't tell where this is going, and we're breaking all sorts of federal laws. We could both go to prison for a very long time. And I'm in it along with you. So yeah, I'm with you but it doesn't mean I'm not going to protest and speak my mind."

"I know we're together on this. I couldn't do it without your programming skills," I said.

"That's exactly what a federal D.A. will assert when we're indicted together for....for what? Espionage? Is that what it is for breaking into the holy grail of U.S. intelligence files?"

"Something' like that. Let's not get caught," I said.

"Sure. But I wish we had some options. What we're doing might be discovered. We think we're obliterating your entries into their sacred data. And we are. At least we are until perhaps someone clever on the other side discovers our program, or at least its effects."

"What do'ya mean? They haven't so far. Where's the exposure? Isn't your program erasing our tracks and self-destructing itself each time?"

"I hope so. But it's like any crime; you can't know when you've left some sort of evidence. If we're clever enough to circumvent such elaborate security and seemingly erase our tracks, then there might be some way for one of their very clever guys to discover us. Or, since the technology advances so rapidly, what isn't possible today suddenly becomes possible and we're suddenly fucked. At any rate, we've come this far so what's next?"

"We're going to give the Guatemalan Military their own 'Felix', their own informer within the CIA. His code name will be 'Dick'. The suggestion is that Dick is working locally out of the U.S. Embassy."

I continued. "Dick singles out two high ranking police commanders. Rivals. Lots of intelligence reports on both. No love-loss between them. We'll set up two wholly fabricated groups working to subvert each other. Dick will request cash payments. We'll notify the other faction about each payment exchange. We'll have people antagonistic to the Government pick up the money. Clear evidence implicating the other group. For one group, I'll use dead drops. For the other, I'll arrange live ex-changes."

"And we'll also give the CIA something to work with. I've located certain drug dealer bank accounts, or I should say the CIA has. Cayman Islands. I can break in. CIA knows the account numbers and passwords. Drug money gets transferred to both senior officers and maybe a few others. The CIA's man at the bank will of course discover these large wire transfers and their origins. Hard to say what the CIA will do. Probably nothing, but it's worth a go. At any rate, we'll also send anonymous info to General Cervantes, the commander of the Military. He'll be pissed for not getting a cut. I've got to be-lieve he'll do something."

"What do'ya think, Angela?"

"I'm impressed with your deviousness. How do we communicate? Can't use e-mail. It's not secure. Or can we?"

"Why not? Can't be traced to us. If it's read, who ca-res? Maybe creates even more chaos."

"How do you open bogus accounts for these police guys?"

"Easy. I simply call someone at the bank. Tell them I'm with the Cayman Islands bank where the transfers will come from. I identify our two victims by name and address. Of course they'll never be challenged to prove their identity because the victims will never know these accounts exist. I then wire transfer a significant sum to open the accounts. No bank refuses deposits."

I was amused and relieved that Angela was now more into the detail rather than wrestling with the moral issues. I began mapping out the plan of attack the next day. The following day I opened accounts at Banco Na-tionale de Guatemala for Colonel Francisco Cordoba and Major Miguel DeOrio of the Internal Security Forces. I could not prove it, but these two senior police officials were the most likely to have ordered the killings of my father and uncle.

The initial transfer was for $20,000 USD each. Sooner or later the drug dealer account I was accessing would eventually identify the irregularity in their balance, but I should have some time. The account saw a large amount of deposit and withdrawal transactions and mine would be lost in the volume. The account balance was always in the tens of millions.

The next day I invented 'Dick'. I used the same e-mail ploy that the return address was a fiction and would change each transmission. The wonders of technology. Even Guatemalan Secret Police have e-mail these days.

Dick told them what he had access to. That he worked for the U.S. What he wanted. As an introduction, I gave each some personal intelligence on the other that I had culled from CIA field reports. Both responded within the week. There was no haggling over Dick's fee. Payment would be on delivery of information.

My first sale of information to these two characters had a foundation based on CIA intelligence reports, but elaborated for increased effect. I thought about a book I read on the great charade perpetrated on the Nazis by the British double agent known as Garbo who created a whole fabricated history populated with fictional characters. Angela and I spent a whole night creating this body of fiction. It proved to be worth $2,000 to each Guatemalan officer. Each was given the time and place for the exchange of their payment as well as information on the payoffs to the other rival officer so that they would investigate and document each other.

Over the next two months I built on this fictitious foundation by creating a history of payments made and received by Colonel Cordoba and Major DeOrio. On the side, I continued to feed my newspaper editor and the opposition leader useful information. Unfortunately, Felix was quiet. No reports had been filed for weeks.

"So what do you think is happening?" Angela asked. We were treating ourselves to a nice dinner on a Friday night.

"Have no idea. Felix has not reported for weeks. The other intelligence reports from CIA operatives are boring and seem remote and vague. Felix is obviously a national. Probably someone on the inside. Either with the Internal Security Forces or maybe some government position with lots of access. His intel is pretty deep."

"Carlos -- why don't we quit this? I'm worried about getting caught."

"We've been over this before, Honey. Besides, we don't even know if we have accomplished anything. Tell you what; we'll just relax this weekend. No making trouble."

It turned out to be a great weekend. Lots of wine. Lots of lovemaking. Tough to get through a dreary Monday. The rest of the week would prove even worse.

As I left the office, two men grabbed me by each arm and propelled me to a car with the door opened by a third man.

"Mister Martin, we're with the FBI. You'll come with us."

"Am I under arrest?"

"Not at this time. However, we do have the authority to detain you under custody on suspicion of violation of the National Secrets Act." I was forced into the back seat of the car and handcuffed.

None of us spoke on the ride to FBI headquarters. I was eventually placed in a room and left alone for half an hour.

Two men entered the room. "Mister Martin, I 'm Special Agent Roger Alexander and this is Special Agent Howell."

"When do I get to call an attorney?"

"Do you have an attorney?"

"When do I get to call an attorney?" I repeated.

"You'll get that opportunity. But let me tell you why you're here. We have evidence that you have been illegally accessing intelligence files at NSA and CIA. Do you have anything to say about that? Things might go better for you if you just tell us what you've been up to."

I was not about to engage him in a discussion. They would love to start a dialogue. That meant they had no good evidence. Just wait them out.

"Could I get some coffee?"

"Later, Mister Martin. We need some information first."

"No. I need to call an attorney first. Or are you saying that I can't go or call an attorney?" It sounded smart-ass even though I was scared shitless. Angela had warned me. I had underestimated security.

Agent Alexander left the room without responding. Agent Howell glowered at me. Within minutes, Alexander returned with another man. Older than the FBI agents and not as fit.

"My name is Carson, Mister Martin. I'm with Central Intelligence. Let me tell you where you are. You're in a pit of shit up to your neck and just about ready to go under. You can help us, or we can give you a shove. We want to know what information you accessed and who you're working for. In exchange, we can work something out to mitigate what is going to happen to you. This is a national security matter so certain legal niceties do not apply."

"All the more reason for me to call an attorney. Been try'in to tell these guys that."

"Ok, Carlos. If that's the way you want to play it. But let me tell you the scenario down that path. The Federal DA will seek an indictment. Guarantee you that will not be difficult. The DA will argue about flight potential. Don't know the potential of your foreign associations. Ethnic ties to a foreign country. National security concerns. Highest security clearance employee. Bottom line is, no bail my friend. You'll be held for a long time while we dig into you. And that sweet girlfriend of yours." There was a clear reaction on my part. "You haven't even asked. She's been detained, too," he said.

After the initial panic of hearing about Angela being picked up, I quickly settled down to dealing with the situation. Angela would manage ok. She was tough and smart. Maybe better prepared for this than me.

"Well Mister Whoever, I still need to get an attorney. Until then, I'm not going to discuss anything."

The CIA guy stared at me briefly then left the room with Agent Alexander. Agent Howell was left to keep me company. Neither of us said anything for the next thirty minutes. Then the door opened and someone came in with a tray of coffee and donuts. Agent Howell and the person with the tray left.

What the hell, I helped myself to coffee. I didn't think that would make me more pliable. At any rate, it was better than sleep deprivation or beatings. After my second cup of coffee, I got into the donuts.

Maybe forty minutes had passed when the door opened again. Agent Alexander was accompanied by two other men I had not previously seen.

Alexander introduced them. "Mister Martin, this is Assistant U.S. District Attorney McCullough, and Mister Goldman."

The slight, five foot five, sixty-year-old man identified as Goldman introduced himself and offered his hand, "Morris Goldman, Mister Martin. I've been retained by Miss Renaldi to represent both of you."

"Where's Angela?"

"She's fine. Sends her love. Like you, she's been detained by the FBI," Goldman answered. I was bewildered how Angela had arranged for an attorney so quickly.

"Mister Martin. We know you have been accessing highly secured files within various databases of the U.S. government. We know you have used your special level of access security as a result of your job duties to access NSA and CIA files. If you are prepared to tell us who you are working for and the details of the information you stole, the Government is prepared to offer you limited immunity and a reduced sentence,"

"Charlie, what have you got? My client isn't going to respond to your open ended, vague allegations," Goldman said. Like a good client, I kept my mouth shut.

"We have technical records of unusual and unauthorized entries into highly classified databases. That trail leads directly, and by exclusion of other staff, only to your client. "

"Technical records? What's that mean? Exclusion? You mean you've seemingly cleared everybody else except my client, so he's it by process of elimination?" Goldman asked.

"I'm not prepared to discuss the details of the evidence, but I'm assured by highly qualified information technology professionals that your client is the source. I might add that these professionals are outside people with heavy credentials, prepared to testify."

"I don't know about you, Charlie, but I don't know much beyond my word-processing and looking for stuff on the Internet. Just what are these technical records? Disks? Hard copies? Printouts of transactions? What?"

McCullough took an audible breath. "The evidence against your client is not so overt. It is highly technical, but no less specific. We have enough to seek an indictment."

"Give me a break, Charlie. That's bullshit. That means you have fuzzy technical stuff that a jury probably won't understand, maybe not even a judge. I'm going to stop this here. You either charge my client right now, or we'll be before Judge Williams tomorrow. And if that doesn't work, how about the Washington Post? You want another Los Alamos, Dr. Lee fiasco on your doorstep? So what's it to be, Charlie? You can formally charge or I'll have a writ within hours."

The D.A. looked at me. "Mister Martin, you're in deep trouble. We have evidence that we think can convict you on a number of federal felony charges. Serious charges that carry long sentences. We are prepared to discuss a reduction in the extent of the charges in exchange for a full disclosure of what you've been doing."

"Too premature to discuss any bargain. You'll have to demonstrate the substance of your evidence first. I'm instructing Mister Martin to say nothing. Charge him or release him, Charlie," Goldman said.

The U.S. District Attorney just stared at me, then at my attorney for a long time before answering. "Morris, this is too serious to just release your client. We will charge him. He'll be charged with at least theft of government property, violation of the National Security Act. Charges might escalate to espionage. He'll be arraigned tomorrow."

"There'll be no further questioning of my client?"

Reluctantly, the D.A. answered, "No. Not without you present, Morris."

"And what about Angela?" I asked.

"We've already released Miss Renaldi. That doesn't mean we won't charge her. The investigation is still ongoing. You were arrested sooner than we would have liked, only to stop your further access into secure government files. It will simply take a little longer to assemble the necessary evidence for trial."

"Can I have some time with my client?" Goldman asked.

"Ok, Morris. Thirty minutes, then he gets formally charged and processed. Professional courtesy."

"This room secure? No sound recording?"

"No recording system, Morris." The D.A. answered. "Thirty minutes." He left and closed the door.

"Who are you Mister Goldman?" I asked.

"Like I said, your Miss Renaldi called me. And by the way, she's released as Mister McCullough indicated. She's downstairs. Now I have a few questions before they book you."

The idea of being jailed hit me like a fist in the stomach.

Goldman continued. "We'll have more time tomorrow. In the mean time you say nothing. But there're a few facts I want to establish."

"Is there any physical evidence at your apartment, or anywhere?"

"What do'ya mean?"

"Carlos. Angela has told me everything. I'm your lawyer, so let's cut through the crap. I'm sure they have already obtained a search warrant. They're probably searching your place as we speak. I need to know what they'll find."

"The disk. Have they got that?"

"You mean with the pornography files? Angela told me how she had rigged the password trap. My guess is that Angela's trap worked and anything incriminating was destroyed. That would be compelling and direct physical evidence. McCullough implied highly technical evidence. The disk would be totally condemning physical evidence, and McCullough wouldn't be hedging."

"You apparently know McCullough. How's that? And how was it that Angela found you?"

"I'm a criminal defense attorney. I've had a lot of experience in government security related cases. As to why Angela contacted me, I asked her that too. She said she'd researched criminal lawyers over the last couple of months. She was apparently covering for a potential eventuality like this. So, is there anything at your apartment?"

"The desk top computer has all my work on it but I think it's probably safe."

"Jesus. You mean you kept all this data you stole on your computer at home?"

"Yeah, but you don't understand. They won't be able to get to it.' I said. At least I hoped they couldn't."

"Carlos, they'll bring in the best IT guys there are. What makes you think you've outsmarted them?"

"First of all, Angela and I are among those *best IT guys*. Angela set three tiers of user names and passwords. If you successfully enter at the first prompt, then you need to hit an icon within ten seconds to call up a second drop down box to enter another password. You repeat a third time. If at any time you fail to correctly enter the second or third password within the ten second limit, all hard disk files are erased."

"And tell me; how failsafe do you think that is?"

"Should be adequate, but the data is also encrypted. The encryption software is parked in an on-line software provider website that I hacked into. I go in and download it each time. The software provider doesn't even know it's there. There's a hard copy CD taped under a reading table at a library. No finger prints."

"I don't understand any of that techno-babble, but I'll hope that you're correct," Goldman said.

"And lastly, if there is any attempt at removing the hard drive, all files are deleted if it's physically disconnected from the computer."

"I guess I can understand that. I'll see you tomorrow, Carlos. I'll also bring Angela."

"Tell her I love her, Mister Goldman."

"I will." Goldman stood, shook hands, then asked, "Do you know if any of your, whatever the word is, scenarios you created ever had any results?"

"A couple of my first ventures."

"What happened?"

I did not want to poison my own attorney against me so I answered vaguely, "I was able to get rid of a colonel and two captains of the Guatemalan police."

The next several weeks passed in a blur. I was formerly arraigned and contrary to the threats, bail was set. Lower than I thought, but it still cost all our savings to cover the ten percent to the bail bondsman. Both Angela and I were of course suspended from our jobs. We had a lot of time and nothing to do but be close.

A week before my scheduled appearance at a preliminary hearing, Angela and I appeared at the Justice Department office of U.S. Assistant Attorney Charles McCullough, and a whole room full of government types from several agencies and our attorney, Morris Goldman.

"Mister Martin, Miss Renaldi," McCullough started the meeting.

"Charlie, Miss. Renaldi has not even been charged. What charges are you considering?"

Having been deflected from his canned speech, McCullough responded in an exasperated tone. "Accessory to all the same charges levied against Mister Martin. But let's get to why we are here. The charges are serious. Violation of the National Secrets Act and theft of government property may only be the start. Espionage may not be out of the question. Miss Renaldi is not out of the woods yet. U.S. interests have been comprised. However, the circumstances have not as yet substantially affected national security. Therefore, the Government is prepared to reduce charges in exchange for full disclosure of the methods of access and the details of all illegal use of the stolen information."

"Reduce charges? You mean full immunity?"

"No. Not immunity. We would reduce Mister Martin's charges to theft of government property, and no charges would be filed against Miss Renaldi."

"Let me talk with my clients," Goldman said. The three of us left the office to caucus in the hallway.

Before I could ask anything, Goldman said to us, "My advice is to settle for nothing less than immunity. I sense their evidence is poor. They might not even get an indictment. They know it's you, Carlos, but they probably have a weak case. They have avoided anything specific, mostly resorting to intimidation. Lastly, have you looked at all those suits in the room? They're other agencies. They only care about finding out how you did it. They'll pressure Justice in return for information. So what do you say?"

I looked at Angela. She shook her head in agreement. We returned to the room.

"My clients decline any offer short of full immunity."

"Not good enough, Morris. Your clients are not going to just walk on this."

"Very well, Charlie. We'll see you in court next week," Goldman answered.

"Mister Goldman, would you and your clients give us a few minutes?" A middle-aged man said without identifying himself. McCullough looked ready to explode.

We returned to the hallway. Seemed undignified but I guess that's what you get when you're a criminal. Ten minutes later we were beckoned back.

"In the interests of national security, my colleagues from other agencies have made a compelling case to offer full immunity against prosecution in exchange for full cooperation," McCullough said with no attempt at concealing his anger.

"Very well, Charlie. Draft it up for us to see. Make it simple and comprehensive. In the meantime I'll talk with my clients again," Goldman said.

Once outside in the hallway, Goldman said, "This should be straightforward. With immunity you can be compelled to testify, no taking the Fifth Amendment. If you don't, they can pursue obstruction of justice charges, or perjury if you testify untruthfully. My advice is to tell them everything. Get this behind you and move on with your lives. And count yourself lucky that you're not both doing a lot of years in a federal penitentiary."

We talked for a few minutes. Both Angela and I agreed to cooperate.

Back inside the conference room, McCullough handed Goldman the immunity agreement.

"What the hell is this clause about agreeing not to engage in any computer software related profession? Those are my clients' marketable skills. You would deprive them of making a living?" Goldman said. "No deal."

"That's standard. Just like any hacker gets. It's the only way we can insure no repeated illegal activities."

"No fucking way. That means any time I touch a computer you assholes could arrest me. Angela, let's go," I said. I started to get out of my chair.

The middle-aged man said, "Strike it, Mister McCullough. Mister Martin and Miss Renaldi won't repeat their crimes. They're too good. So good, that anything resembling a repeat of their escapades would be like a signature. Isn't that correct Mister Martin?"

"Right," I answered.

McCullough struck the paragraph and initialed the change. He nearly flung the copies back to Morris Goldman.

"Seems in order. Let me explain it to my clients."

"The government commits to no prosecution on any charges related to the acquisition and use of any U.S. Government information governed by the National Security Act prior to this date. The granting of this immunity is contingent upon Carlos Martin and Angela Rinaldi cooperating fully with any government agency designated by the Justice Department to number one, explain in detail all methods of illegal access of electronic information and circumvention of security measures; secondly, to provide details of where and to whom information was disseminated; and thirdly, to agree not to divulge to anyone the nature of their acts in any way whatsoever. The U.S. District Attorney has signed for the government. Each of you needs to sign a copy."

"I have one condition," I said. Morris Goldman glared at me. He did not like surprises from clients. "They killed my father and uncle. I want to know what has happened."

"What the hell does that mean?" McCullough blurted out.

"It means I want to know what has happened in Guatemala," I said.

"No deal. It's fine with me if you don't sign, Mister Martin. Sign it or we'll have you before a federal judge!" McCullough shouted.

The same middle-aged man responded immediately, "Mister McCullough, we have no problem in satisfying Mister Martin's curiosity as to the consequences of his actions. We've come this far. You can amend the agreement accordingly."

"Fine. I assume you will agree to a hand-written amendment Mister Goldman?" Before Goldman could answer, McCullough had grabbed our two copies of the agreement and scrawled an amendment. The verbiage said in effect that we would be advised of the consequences of our illegal acts.

"If that's all Mister McCullough, then we would like to start debriefing right away," the middle aged man said. McCullough simply nodded.

Angela, Goldman, and I were ushered to another conference room. On the other side of a long table were FBI, CIA, NSA, State Department, and Justice Department, along with a couple of contract computer experts, and a stenographer. The middle-aged man apparently in charge was a senior FBI official.

We spent the next five hours starting to explain the technical aspects of our attack into the government databases. It was a long session for those in the room that were not information technology experts. At this level, the discussion was probably incomprehensible to them.

The debriefings continued for the next four weeks almost every day. Once we got past the technical explanations we started to discuss where the information went. True to their deal, the Government told us what they knew about any consequences of our deceptions. At least we assumed they were telling us what happened, but it could have been fiction.

Major DeOrio was murdered, assailants unknown.

Colonel Cordoba had been arrested under presidential order and was now in a military prison awaiting trial.

The 'good' Colonel Melendez was promoted past other generals to take command of the Military replacing General Cervantes. Cervantes committed 'suicide'. The CIA assumed that Melendez ordered the killing. Angela and I were pointedly accused of diminishing U.S. influence in Guatemala since Melendez was a strong critic of the U.S. Speculation was that the President was forced to promote Melendez or risk a military coup.

Under Melendez, all senior officers in the Internal Security Forces were changed and a trusted Melendez protégé placed in command. Probably still no guarantee that police abuses would not continue.

Intelligence reports suggested that the militant opposition group that received my intelligence had indeed acted on it. With several killings and other attempts on individual police, the police had lately withdrawn to barracks.

Not from the CIA, but from the U.S. newspapers we learned that Senator Campbell, Chairman of the Foreign Relations Committee, was calling for hearings on the role of U.S. Military and U.S. Intelligence in Guatemala. We did not tell them of our direct feed of information to the Senator. I suggested to the FBI and CIA that Campbell probably had strong sources in Guatemala. The Senator's e-mails were factiously addressed from the opposition leader Senior Villalobos. There had been a fairly vigorous exchange as I funneled CIA intelligence directly to the Senator.

I am sure the Senator thought Villalobos was arrested or killed when the e-mail exchange stopped with my arrest. The CIA was in for some tough questioning on the Hill.

After almost three months of exhaustive debriefing, Mr. Johnson our middle aged FBI guy in charge concluded with what we had been told should be our last debriefing session.

"Both you and Miss Renaldi have been most cooperative. And I hope you felt we fulfilled our part of the bargain by telling you the details of the damage you caused. With that said, I want to make a personal statement."

"You two have taken it upon yourselves to interfere in sensitive areas of your Country's foreign policy. You have no idea what damage you have caused. You feel satisfied with the people that have been killed? In my opinion, you're part of that vast group of naïve people that see foreign policy in emotional and simplistic terms. I have nothing but contempt for both of you. But you probably could care less about what I think."

After a pause, Johnson continued. "We're going to part company here today. But I cannot let you off that easily. You'll be hearing from the Government again soon. You see, you have violated laws within the Republic of Guatemala. Our legal experts also believe there is potential in filing charges with the International War Crimes Tribunal for human rights violations. After all, you directly caused the deaths of several people through what amounts to electronic terrorism. We also suspect you provided Senator Campbell with classified materials and did not divulge that fact, therefore violating the terms of your immunity agreement."

"What the fuck are you talking about?" I screamed.

"You and your girlfriend killed Guatemalan government officials through illegal actions. Acts of terrorism I should say. Simple as that. I believe that an international arrest warrant might be forthcoming."

"You are assholes. You've been living so long in your own internalized shit that you don't represent anything anymore, except the FBI. Come on Angela, let's get the fuck out of here," I said.

"Before we go, Carlos. I need to confess something to Mister Johnson," Angela said.

"You don't need to tell this asshole anything," I said.

Angela continued. "Well, this is important for everybody to know. You especially, Mister Johnson. I was always worried about something going wrong. So I created elaborate mechanisms to prevent any evidence being discovered. Obviously not good enough. I researched a good lawyer just in case, one with the necessary security clearance so he could represent us. I also thought about creating a bargaining chip to trade in case it all went wrong. With the immunity agreement, I thought that was behind us. Since it apparently isn't, then now's the time to trade," Angela said.

I had no idea where she was going with these comments.

"What are you talking about?" Johnson asked.

"I'm talking about my bomb, Mister Johnson."

"Bomb? What the hell do you mean?" Johnson stiffened bolt upright.

"Oh! Sorry. Not a bomb that kills people. A bomb that kills databases," Angela said. "It was a just-in-case."

"And just what the hell are you talking about, Miss Renaldi?"

"Well. I'm talking about the software equivalent of a biological weapon. A virus. A very bad virus. A virus that will destroy or contaminate not just one, but any of the databases that Carlos accessed with our entry program. And by the way, if your experts discover the code, I suggest they not tamper with it since it is booby trapped. The damage would be immense."

Johnson stared at Angela for several moments. He was flushed with rage. "You miserable pieces of shit. If I could have you killed, I'd do it in a heartbeat. You're enemies of this Country. So tell me about this virus bomb. What's the game?"

"What's there to tell, Mister FBI? We had a deal, now you're trying to fuck us. You can take your patriotic shit and stuff it up your ass. Better yet, take this virus and stuff it up your ass," Angela screamed at Johnson. I had never seen this side of Angela, black with anger.

After a couple of deep breaths, she continued, "The game as you put it is complete immunity about anything having to do with this affair. No, I'll make it clearer since you lawyer pricks like to find loopholes. The immunity will cover any fucking thing either one of us did. No qualifications. Federal jaywalking, pissing in public, whatever. You'll get us a new document from McCullough or the bomb will go off. Or maybe I'm bluffing. Tough call isn't it? And since there are no witnesses to this conversation, you'll find it hard to prosecute us on damaging your sacred files. And there will be massive damage. I don't even know how far it could spread. And you'll never know if you've gotten rid of it. You know how good I am. Threat's real. So what's it to be Mister Johnson?"

I had never seen Angela like this. She actually grinned at Johnson. She was vicious beyond anything I had ever seen. I assumed it was the sense of betrayal that set her off.

Johnson pulled in his horns. "The timing?"

"Soon. I suggest a comprehensive immunity agreement be drafted real soon. How soon? Let's say within a couple of days. Since you haven't asked, the bomb goes off if I don't go in and disable it by a certain date."

"You understand we'll need to see how you disable your bomb," Johnson said.

"Jesus, you guys are a piece of work," Angela responded. "Yeah, sure, I'll show your expert assholes some real creativity."

A bewildered U.S. Attorney McCullough delivered a new and simple immunity agreement that covered virtually any federal crime prior to our date of arrest. Morris Goldman was equally surprised. Angela went to CIA headquarters in Langley, Virginia for two hours to disable her very real computer virus bomb. I couldn't have been prouder of her.

Two months after this ordeal, Angela Renaldi and I were married. We moved to California, which seemed as far away as possible from Washington. We each make six figure salaries with high tech firms. A lot of that goes to our house on the upper San Francisco Bay in Sausalito. We 'virtually commute', driving down to San Jose only once a week.

Neither of us misses Washington. Neither of us forgets Guatemala.

THE END

By Douglas Clark

"As a burning and a fever
Which could cling to thee forever.
Now are thoughts that shalt not banish –
Now are visions ne'er to vanish."
  Edgar Allen Poe, Spirits of the Dead

It was October, there was a light chill in the air as the middle-aged man and a younger woman sat on a patio in the south of France sharing a bottle of wine. The large early nineteenth century stone farmhouse was located outside the quaint wine town of Châteauneuf-du-Pape in Provence. It sat back off a secondary road surrounded by trees with views of vineyards and olive groves spreading out in all directions. The Rhone River was two miles in the distance. The leaves on the grapevines had turned hews of yellows and reds.

"All right, Elliot, are you going to tell me why you insisted I fly here to see you?" Allison Kryszka said. She was an elegant young woman, dressed impeccably. She had arrived just a few hours ago by the high-speed train from Paris to Avignon in Provence.

Elliot Gaston looked to be around sixty. Fit and tanned. Good head of gray hair. Average build. Dressed in casual attire of cotton shirt and chinos, the sleeves of a sweater draped over his shoulders. He looked typical Provencal.

"Certainly, Allison. I'm sorry that I've been so cloak and dagger about wanting you to come here. Let me first say that you are my most trusted friend. No, you're more than a friend." He reached over and took her hand. "What I'm about to tell you will dismay you. You also will not believe me, at least at first. Hopefully I can convince you. That's why I needed to talk to you here. Somewhat captive. But is it not magnificent?" He said sweeping his hand to the surrounding view.

"Yes it is, Elliot, but now you have me worried. Tell me what this is about."

Still holding her hand he said, "Allison --- I've been diagnosed with terminal cancer, leukemia actually."

She grabbed his hand with both of her hands and started to cry. "God, no. Are they sure? It's not treatable?"

Gaston gently touched her cheek and attempted to wipe her tears with a handkerchief. "I'm afraid so, Allison. I've been to the best oncologists in Paris. It's known as acute myelogenous leukemia. It has an 85% mortality rate. I've been receiving chemotherapy for a couple of months. Unfortunately, the therapy has not put the cancer in remission, and the side effects are dreadful. It's been a couple of weeks since my last treatment that's why I look normal. But I didn't bring you all this way just to tell you about my impending mortality. There's something more I must explain."

"Damnit, Elliot, you're too talented to die. You're too young. What are you, sixty?" Allison said,

Elliot Gaston paused for several moments and looked into her eyes. "No, I'm not sixty. That's what's at issue here. That's what I need to explain. I'm much older. You won't believe what I am about to tell you, but that's why I wanted you here, so I can convince you."

"What do you mean? So you're sixty-five? More?"

Elliot sighed and answered, "Much more than that I'm afraid. Allison, I was born in 1873."

Allison Kryszka stared at him for several moments, before responding. "What the hell's that supposed to mean, Elliot?"

"Well I don't know how to say it any other way. I assure you that I'm not deranged. I know it's not seemingly possible, but it is, Allison. I've lived every minute of those years. Here, this will help with the details."

Elliot placed a three-inch thick manuscript on the table. "It's a first draft. Needs more work. It's the story of my life. I want it to be more than a just a journal or a memoir. I want anyone reading it to see my unusual journey. Considering my situation, I wanted you to see it and start the process of believing."

Allison shook her head slowly and stood up. "I don't know what you're trying to do, Elliot, but it's pretty shitty to drag me all this way to France to play whatever game this is." She was angry and paced about with her hands on her hips.

"It's not a game, Allison. I would never do that to you."

"I don't know what to say, Elliot. I've always thought you to be this erudite man of the world. Now this comes out of the blue. You seem rational, but you're asking me to dispel common sense. What makes you think that you are not just imagining this?" There was still anger in her voice.

"Listen, Allison, all I ask is that you spend a couple of days here to let me try to convince you. Right now, let's go inside and I'll prepare us some dinner. I've become a passable cook these last years. Limited repertoire, but what I can do is pretty good."

Elliot seated Allison at the kitchen table and refilled her wine glass. He then lit a fire in the massive fireplace in the adjacent family room. While Elliot busied himself preparing dinner, Allison moved the conversation away from his disturbing assertion about his age.

The house was quite magnificent. The walls were of great stone, and twelve-inch thick exposed beams supporting the weighty slate roof. Elliot told her that it was built around 1820. He spent a couple of years renovating and modernizing the plumbing and kitchen. Between keeping an eye on dinner, he would guide her around the rooms explaining the house's linage and construction. The conversation was light as Elliot talked about living and writing in Provence, drawing in Allison to talk about the contrasts with her living in New York.

"This is an absolutely charming house, Elliot. Too clean for a bachelor. How do you manage?"

"I have a wonderful couple of housekeepers, two old-maid sisters, Antoinette and Pauline," Elliot said. "They've adopted me. The day they come in to clean, that evening they prepare dinner and the three of us enjoy a couple bottles of wine. I am sure that it's a special part of their social life. I tease them that there must be a local rumor about our being a threesome."

Elliot opened another bottle of wine and sat down at the table. "Where to start?" he said as much to himself as to his longtime literary agent. "I don't want to discuss the cancer. That's secondary right now, Allison."

Allison sat silently, disoriented by all that her favorite client had told her. The anger had abated but she still didn't know how to gauge Elliot's wild claim to absurd longevity.

Elliot said, "Have you ever wondered how I've been so successful with my novels of the early part of the twentieth century? Why the critics say that I am able to evoke an uncanny sense of feeling for the time?"

"You're talented," Allison said. "You have an astounding knowledge of history. Others have had success writing about previous times."

"Not many. Any come to mind? The good literature was mostly written by those of that time. Most writings about earlier times are biographical or more historical in concept. Novels are more rare. Mine are more about the people. How they lived and felt. *Why* they felt the way they did. Too show, not to tell the reader what it was like during those earlier times, especially the difficult times."

"So you're saying it's because you lived those times? That you're somehow immortal?"

Elliot answered, "Not immortal, Allison. Remember, I have a terminal disease. I've had broken bones. I bleed. I get sick. I just don't age at the same rate everyone else does."

"Every woman would hope for that," Allison said. She smiled and then said more seriously, "I'll admit that for the eighteen years I have known you, you don't look any older."

Elliot pulled his French passport from his pocket and handed it to her. "Take a look at the birth date, Allison."

See looked at the passport, then looked back to Elliot with a puzzled look. "It says you were born in 1928. That makes you in your late seventies. Absurd enough since you look twenty years younger, but I thought you said you were born in 1873?"

"I was. But with my *problem* I had to acquire a new identity at some point. I'll expand on those details later. As you can imagine, even now I'm experiencing some problems of incredulity if anyone checks my date of birth when I need to show ID. Take a look at these," Elliot said as he handed Allison an envelope.

She opened the envelope and spilled out a dozen photographs. All were black and white. They were cracked and dog-eared.

"Recognize me?" Elliot said as Allison looked at each photograph.

"I guess. The young boy could be you. The others do appear to be you. They're old photos, or at least they look old," she said.

"Come on, Allison. Do you think I'd fake these? Try to deceive you? That would make me raving mad or a charlatan." Elliot said. " Look at them again."

Somewhat subdued, Allison asked, "Why are you telling me this, Elliot? What is it you want me to do?"

"Just listen to my story. I want to tell you about the major events that shaped my life. And about times that shaped our world today. About a wisdom that could only come from my unique longevity. Along the way, I hope to give you enough evidence for you to believe what I say is true. Enough for you to get this work published. And published as non-fiction."

And so began the first part of Elliot Gaston-Dillan Murphy's story.

Excerpt from *The Journal Of Dillan Murphy* – Eastern Pennsylvania, 1876-1898

My real name is Dillan Murphy. I was born March thirty-first, 1873. I was of Irish ancestry. My grandfather immigrated to America in 1846, from County Mayo in the west of Ireland with my grandmother and my father. It was the first disastrous year of the Great Potato Famine in Ireland, killing or driving out enormous numbers of the poor threatened with starvation or disease. My grandfather took a job in the coalmines in Pennsylvania. With little other opportunities, my father eventually followed him into the mines at age seventeen.

We lived in Schuylkill County, Pennsylvania. My mother died when I was three, probably from cancer, but back in that period it wasn't as easily diagnosed. According to my father, once she fell ill and took to her bed, she passed on in a matter of months.

My father told me some years later that he would never have gone on after her death if it hadn't been for me. He had married comparatively late in life for back then. Wanting a better life for his future family than his fellow miners, he saved as much money as possible before courting my mother. When they married, he had a small home set on a couple of acres. He was in his late thirties and she was in her early twenties. They were both devoted to each other as much from intellectual an attachment as from the emotional bond. A year later I was born, and was to be their only child.

My father was strict about my education. Unlike many others my age from miner families, he saw to it that I always attended school. Although uneducated himself, he could read and he loved books. When I was around ten years old, I remember him saying to me, probably because I was not being as serious as I should with my studies, "Son, let me tell you about a promise I made to your mother just before she passed on. I promised her that you'd never go into the mines. It's a terrible life. It killed your granddad, and it'll be killin' me 'fore long. You work in the dark and damp. You're breathin' dust that will shorten your life, that's if you don't get killed in some accident first. I've got the black lung my-self. Don't know how many more years I have."

My father was strongly pro-union. He likened the Pennsylvania mine owners to English and Scottish land-holders in Ireland, making their wealth in agriculture on the backs of poor tenant farmers. They had turned their backs on the plight of their starving serfs during the Great Potato Famine. In like kind, the mine owners held the workforce in economic bondage with the *company store* concept, and then forced them into unsafe mines. There was many a night that he was out late. With no mother, I was home alone. I remember being terribly worried and unable to sleep until his return.

Because of his politics, I asked him once if he was a member of the secret organization, the Molly Maquires. Everyone knew of the Molly Maguire's. They were a vio-lent group of Irish immigrants in Schuylkill County that pitted themselves against the mine owners in the early days of labor union organization. Today the Mollies might be labeled terrorists. To the miserable coal miner families, there was a romantic aura in their resistance to the powerful mine owners.

"No I'm not, Son. I'm for the Unions, but I'm not for the murderin' ways of the Mollies. They're no different than the greedy bastards that own the collieries and they only make it tougher on us Irish." Even so, he knew a surprising lot about the Molly Maquires, perhaps too much I speculated.

The background for my novel, *Color Me Black,* was largely autobiographical coming from listening and watching my father and his fellow miners. The Molly Macquire protagonist came straight out of the environ-ment I knew.

I remember that conversation because I was jarred by his revelation of impending mortality. He went on to tell me, "And the only way out for you my Son is to get an education. That means hard work at your studies. And I don't mean just secondary school. I mean going on to university. We live tightly because I always put away as much as I can towards your education. When you're of age in a few years, there'll be enough to get you started."

I didn't even know of anyone that attended a university other than the village doctor. Getting an education at a university became both of our focus. We talked every evening about the future. My father and I discussed history, philosophy, and science. I wondered what he might have done had he not been trapped in poverty. He became my best friend. We shared things beyond the interest or understanding of my schoolmates.

I came from very humble beginnings, but rich in my father's love, and rich in intellectual stimulation. It was a singularly unique life, totally at odds with my environment. By the time I was in secondary school, my teachers recognized a student that was very different from his peers. My peers recognized that also. Since I was *different*, there were a lot of fights. I got the worst of many of those until a fellow miner friend of my father's taught me how to box.

Charles Fergus was a small young miner who augmented his income through wagers with pick-up, bare-knuckle fights. He got takers because of his slight stature, and there were always new miners coming into the area to provide him fresh opportunities.

"Boxin' is all in your head, Lad. If you've good reflexes, you can learn to handle yourself, at least good enough not to get the shit beat out of you," he said. "I'll teach you some moves and how to 'read' the other guy. Boxin' is one thing, but street fightin' is another. I'll teach you some of that too."

Charles Fergus did just that. In exchange for my father teaching him to read, he taught me how to fight. He did a good job and I was a good pupil. Fergus' principal admonition was to first protect your own nose, then go for the other guy's. A shot to the nose was the quickest way to end a fight according to Fergus.

After inflicting a couple of broken noses among several tormentors, it wasn't long before no one was picking on me. I got to the point where I was getting a little cocky and aggressive until what I thought was a big dumb farm boy turned out not to be as slow as I thought. After that lesson, I reserved my skills for defense only.

So when I turned seventeen, I went off to study at Columbia University in New York City. It was Columbia College at the time. It was 1890. I guess I chose Columbia because it was as much different from the rural coalfields of Pennsylvania as possible. Since I liked the written word, I studied journalism figuring it had the most potential for adventure and maybe travel. I'd also confess to being drawn to the power of the newspaper. Here the voice of the people could bring down politicians and denounce corruption. Or at least that was my naivety.

At college, I learned first hand about class distinction based upon wealth. I was the poor kid from the rural working class. I worked nights at a restaurant cleaning tables and washing dishes to support myself. There was no shortage of snobbery among my fellow classmates. I recall no real friends, probably because of my defenses. Hard work at my studies developed an intellectual arrogance to counter my lack of means. It was not a fond time.

My hard work paid off with a professor recommending me for a position with the *New York Herald*. It was James Gordon Bennett's newspaper, the malevolent publisher who had sent Henry Morton Stanley to find the famous Dr. David Livingston in the unexplored regions of East Africa in the eighteen-seventies. Every aspiring journalist hoped for such a great opportunity as Bennett had given to Stanley.

But my job was much more modest and closer to home. One of my assignments was to cover the story of Theodore Roosevelt's efforts to raise a regiment of volunteers to fight in Cuba. I knew Roosevelt from several years of crime reporting. He was the President of the Board of Police Commissioners for New York. Roosevelt had been Assistant Secretary of the Navy before resigning his office to take the lieutenant colonelcy of a newly forming volunteer cavalry regiment.

As so much in life happens simply because of chance circumstances, so was this event in mine.

After giving an interview to a group of reporters, I followed Roosevelt out of the hotel whereupon I asked him, "How does one join up with your regiment, Mister Roosevelt?"

Roosevelt stopped and looked at me with his fabled intensity, "I know you. You're one of Bennett's reporters?"

"Yes, Sir. Been reporting for the *Herald* for several years."

"Well what skills do you have young man? This is a cavalry regiment you know. Can you ride? Can you shoot?"

Neither, I thought to myself, but answered, "Well, I can write and I can box. I can lick any man with my fists in your regiment, Sir." He wasn't sure that was true.

Roosevelt responded, "Well bully for you, young man. I know something of those endeavors as well. And your name, Sir?"

"Murphy, Dillan Murphy."

"Yes, I've read your bylines. First class reporting. I shall request that Mister Gordon make you a war correspondent and attach you to my regiment. Might take a little pressure because your publisher is a notorious tightwad and he probably has already assigned a reporter to accompany our adventure. Since the *Herald* is focused only on New York City, I shall tell him that you are particularly qualified to report on the forthcoming war from the perspective of New York City's interests."

That's the origin of how I followed the First United States Volunteer Cavalry to Cuba in the Spanish-American War. Because the regiment's composition was largely of western rough adventurers, they soon became known as the *Rough Riders*.

■ ■ ■ ■ ■ ■ ■ ■ ■ ■

Elliot interrupted his narrative. They had finished the bottle of wine "It's time for dinner." He rose and retreated to the cellar for another bottle of wine.

Upon his return Allison said, "What you are saying is that you knew Theodore Roosevelt? That would be around the turn of the century?"

"1898 to be exact."

She continued, "So you were in New York in the eighteen-nineties? Tell me what it was like." Her intonation suggesting she was patronizing him but not yet buying into this longevity story.

Elliot was pleased that she was testing him rather than just dismissing him as unhinged. "I've not been back to New York for decades. Obviously, the lack of automobiles was the most striking difference. But what I remember most vividly of New York at the turn of the last century are the bad smells. Garbage, horse waste on the streets, the sewers, unwashed bodies. Pungent smells assaulted one incessantly a hundred years ago."

"No, describe places I would recognize today," she said.

"Very good, I shall tell you a little about New York back in those days, but only after dinner. We are having gnocchi, with a typical Provencal *daube de sanglier,* or wild boar stew. Boars abound in the area. It's a lean meat with only a slight gamy flavor. I do like my French stews."

After dinner he cleared the dishes and settled with Allison in front of the fireplace. Coffee and a fire countered the slight chill coming from the autumn night. "So what do you want to know about New York of a hundred years ago?' Elliot asked knowing Allison was quizzing him.

"What about Midtown Manhattan, around Times Square?" she said.

"As I was saying, if you were to go back in time to the eighteen-nineties, the first thing to strike you about New York would be an assault of smells. Most of them bad. You had the sewers; you had coal being used for heating; you had the elevated railroads spewing all manner of soot and noise from fifty feet up. But at the street level, you had the horses."

"You see, the first subway route wouldn't happen until well after the turn of the century. What you had were horse-drawn trolleys and horse drawn omnibuses. All over town you had continuous piles of fetid horse dung. It would make your eyes water in the summer heat. In winter, steam rose from the piles."

"As for Midtown, what is today's Times Square was a great barnyard that housed the majority of these horses used for public transportation. It was actually located on the southern half of the so-called bow-tie islands created by Broadway and Seventh Avenue. And it smelled like a stock yard."

"It didn't become Times Square until the New York Times built a new building on the horse yards about the same time that the first subway was constructed. Around the turn of the century, Forty-Second Street was the northern end of the City's business district at the time. "

"So was Central Park like it is today?" Allison asked.

"Pretty much. I think it was constructed about the time of the Civil War."

Allison stifled a yawn.

"I agree, my Dear. It's been a long day for you and I also confess to the effects of so much wine. Let's get a good night's sleep. I'll continue my story in the morning after our coffee," he said.

The next morning was warm and the hills suffused with bright sunshine. It was an idyllic setting on the patio with the old stone walled house in perfect composition with the surrounding countryside of an olive grove and distant vineyards. Elliot had prepared coffee and crois-sants.

"I don't want to recite my whole life's story or I'd be talking for weeks. What I want to try to tell you is about my coming of age. My loss of innocence. America's loss of innocence. My journey through the twentieth cen-tury."

Excerpt from *The Journal Of Dillan Murphy* – Cuba, 1898

This is not intended as a history lesson, but I do need to put America's adventurism into context. At the turn of the twentieth century, the United States had defined the forty-eight contiguous states by buying or coercing the western areas from France, Mexico, and Spain. The U.S. was becoming a major industrial power and there was a clear national mood to expand its influence. This nation-alistic fervor became directed at Cuba just ninety miles off the coast of Florida. A populace insurgency against the repressive colonial rule of the Spanish proved to be a rallying cry for U.S. imperialistic expression.

The U.S. battleship *Maine* was dispatched to Havana harbor. She sank after a mysterious explosion killing 250 American sailors. The disaster probably resulted from an accident, but public outcry in America blamed the Spanish. Sixty days later, the U.S. Congress gave President McKinley a declaration of war.

And so it was that young men from all walks of life flocked to join the military ranks. Prospective enlistees for Roosevelt's First United States Volunteer Cavalry Regiment were ten times more than the allotted regimental strength. Even educated men were eager to join the ranks. I was no different. This was a great adventure. Individual aspirations were inseparable from the Nation's ambitions.

I joined the Regiment in Tampa, Florida just two weeks before disembarkation for Cuba. They were a curious collection of hard men from the West and Eastern aristocrats. They were a glorious group of men, each with his reason for going to war.

I fit the same mold. This was to be a great personal adventure. After several years reporting on crime and politics in New York City, the lure of armed conflict in the exotic Caribbean was heady stuff.

I hope that I have enriched my written story with the details and names of some of the wonderful and interesting characters. That was the good part. My first experience of combat was anything but good. I suppose there are those that might find the experience rewarding. Certainly Teddy Roosevelt did. Some of the troopers were ex-lawmen, ex-gunfighters from the Old West who had faced death many times before. For them it was maybe different. For most of us, the experience was terrifying. It was only exhilarating in retrospect.

Our regiment engaged in some minor skirmishing with the Spanish before we moved to the major engagement of taking of the city of Santiago. My first taste of real battle was the Regiment's participation in taking San Juan Hill, or what we called Kettle Hill. Not much of a hill even by eastern Pennsylvania standards, but the Spanish were well entrenched in defensive positions.

It was frightfully hot with a repressive humidity that made every breath an effort. My shirt and trousers were soaked with sweat. My feet sloshed in liquid inside my boots. Too hot even for the mosquitoes, but they would be back in force at nighttime to complete the torment.

I attached myself to a Sergeant Fuller who seemed to be in command of at least his own survival in this tropical pesthole.

"Tell me Sergeant, why'd you join up for this?" I asked as the troop rested. The regiment was dismounted except for the officers. Seemed an odd use of cavalry to me.

"You're a New York feller I hear. Why'd you come, Mister Murphy?"

"Bored with the big city. Adventure in an exotic place. A warm place," I said, smiling with the irony.

He scratched the stubble on his jaw. "Guess it's the same with me. Been a soldier, been a lawman, been a farmer. Farming was boring and it didn't work out, so I'm back solderin'."

We had that brief chat about an hour before I saw Sam Fuller take a bullet in the eye and fall dead next to me. We had been taking fire from the Spanish defenses for several minutes as we advanced through trees and tall grass. The Spanish Regulars fired their Mausers in volleys, the rounds making a buzzing noise because of their great number.

"We'll be fucked this day," a trooper by the name of O'Neil said as he passed and looked down at Sergeant Fuller.

Not everyone was fucked that day, but Trooper O'Neil did foretell his own fate. I was hunkered down with him in the tall grass, which was the only cover we had. Later I determined that TR was credited with moving troops from various regiments out of the exposed areas where we were taking fire from the Spanish firing down on us from trenches on the hill.

Our captain rallied the men forward from atop his horse. From fifty yards away I saw an artillery shell burst above him and the shrapnel tear off his left arm. I remember the horror on his face as he looked at the blood squirting out of the severed stub, probably realizing it foretold his death as well.

As the troop rose up to advance, O'Neil was hit in the lower abdomen. It was an ugly wound, not the clean type of wound usually made by the steel-jacketed Mauser round. O'Neil was literally holding his intestines in his hands. I knelt beside him.

"Well I'm truly fucked good. Will ya do me a favor?"

Of course I said I would as I tucked his bedroll under his head.

"Write my ma and pa. Las Cruces, New Mexico. Tell 'em I did my duty. Tell 'em I died well."

I don't know what O'Neil meant about dying well from such a painful wound that probably took hours to extinguish his life. I returned to his body after the battle ceased. I sat with dead Billy O'Neil awhile and wrote of this day in my journal.

The taking of San Juan Hill was no great thing as most battles go, but there were a lot of Rough Riders that fell that day. Death in war is still death no matter the battle. I had come to know many of these fine men as my friends. I still ponder on their reasons for joining in this fight to risk life and limb in such a contrived war. But then again, my own reasons to risk my life in pursuit of a story might seem just as curious to them.

. . . .

"Let's take a walk, then we'll drive into town to have lunch." Elliot said as he rose from his chair to stretch.

As they strolled next to an olive grove, Allison asked Elliot, "You skipped a lot about your personal life. You say you were born in 1873. So you were twenty-five when you were in Cuba. Was there a wife? A girlfriend?"

"Not exactly, Allison. There were a lot of girls, but no one that I fell in love with. I was arrogant and too full of myself at the time. Regretfully I admit to being what during the times would have been called a despoiler of young women. Although in retrospect, most were already 'spoiled' when I had my liaisons."

"You hear about the sexual repression of the Victorian Era. Was that really the case?" Allison asked.

"Only in the degree to which people discussed sex, which they didn't. As far as actual sexual relations, my personal experiences suggested it was no different than today," Elliot answered.

"So who were these girls that you seduced? Or did some seduce you? Were they *good* girls?" Allison asked.

"All sorts I guess. But if you mean were they *loose* women, I'd say not. Most just followed their desires and ignored the conventions of the time. Like anything else that society prohibits, its value is raised by that prohibition."

"So where did you meet girls a hundred years ago?"

"Single women didn't frequent bars during that era so you had to be creative to find opportunities other than the workplace. Church picnics were the best."

"Church picnics? You mean you would go to church picnics for the express purpose of picking up girls?" Allison laughed.

"Listen, I told you I was no saint. My foraging, I guess you'd call it that, gravitated to those young women aspiring to higher education, especially those associated with the suffrage movement. They were the independent thinkers, which I liked. But self-servingly, they were also the ones to reject the sexual repression of the times, which proved convenient. You must remember this was a time that women did not even have the vote. Many women, particularly those at university, were feeling rebellious. Perhaps as part of that rebellion, they were more persuasive to sexual adventure."

She was still smiling at Elliot's slight embarrassment. "So how about comparing sexual practices of a hundred years ago?"

Elliot grinned. "My narrative is not for the purpose of discussing the titillating details of sexual practices during the early part of the twentieth century."

"And why not, Elliot? If I'm to embrace your story I need details, I need to understand the times," Allison joked. "But I'd rather you told me more about your lovers from that time. Was there someone special?"

Elliot was quiet for several moments and looked down. "Yes there was. After returning from Cuba, I took up reporting again in New York. The next several years were spent advancing my career as a reporter. I became quite good at what later became known as investigative reporting. I was one hell of a muckraker."

"I assume that was the origin of your book, *New York Beat*"? Allison asked.

"Yes. I tried to give a sense of organized crime and corruption in that early part of the century. Political corruption was more than a problem back then. It was the way things were done. At the top of the scale, every municipal contract involved bribes and kickbacks. At the lower levels, most cops were on the take. I became very good at exposing all manner of official corruption. Had a knack for putting the pieces together and mining information from those with a grudge. My success was measured by the number of enemies I made."

Allison interrupted, "Tell me about this first love of your life."

"Very well. Her name was Eleanor, Eleanor Kilpatrick. Irish. And yes she had red hair. She was a beauty. The actress Maureen O'Hara reminded me of Eleanor. You know, the high cheek bones and the fiery eyes," Elliot said.

"And how'd you meet her?"

"At the morgue," Elliot answered.

"The morgue?"

"You see Eleanor was studying medicine and worked nights at the morgue. I was following up on a murder. It involved dismemberment and I was going to try to bribe my way in with a photographer to get photos. Well I ran into Eleanor. First thing I saw was this woman in a particularly bloody apron. The second was her magnificent face. The third was the bite of her acid tongue as she berated me for my antics."

Allison chuckled and Elliot continued, brightened by the memory. "Well I was pretty glib, so I was not only able to appease her, but to my surprise I also got her to agree to lunch the next day."

Elliot filled the next hour telling Allison all the remembrances of his romance with Eleanor Kilpatrick, even titillating her with some of their sexual escapades. Eleanor cared nothing for convention. She also had a healthy sexual appetite.

"But it ended. I guess no different than so many people do. A misunderstanding. At least I thought that to be the reason. It had to do with a certain prostitute."

"A prostitute? You mean Eleanor had a *misunderstanding* about you and a prostitute? You'd better explain that one, Elliot."

"Well you see I was very good at digging out dirt on politicians and other shady characters because I played one low-life against another. I passed out my share of money to get information, but my best results came from playing on rivalries and hatreds. Some of my best sources of information were prostitutes. I was amazed by the level of either their compassion or their hatred for many of their customers," he said.

"So what happened that caused you to lose Eleanor? Didn't she know what kind of work you did?" Allison asked.

"She knew I was a newspaper reporter covering crime and politics. I never told her about the danger and the kinds of people I interacted with. At any rate, there was this prostitute by the name of Francis. One of my best sources. She hated cops and politicians and had a fair number of them as regulars. So one night I'm working this bar trying to get this guy drunk who's a clerk at some city contractor's office so he can do a little spying for me, when in comes Francis."

"Francis is disheveled, dress is torn. She goes to the bar and orders a whiskey. A few minutes later this fat guy barges in and yells, 'Where's that fucking whore?' He's raging drunk and some big guy, obviously a lackey, is with him."

"I recognized him as the local alderman for the district since I knew all the local politicians. He saw Francis and moved toward her, grabbed her by the arm, then backhanded her across the face. 'You fucking whore, I'm goin' to kick the shit out of you so bad nobody'll be fucking you for weeks.'

"Francis was on the floor as I stepped between her and the alderman. 'Who the fuck are you?' the guy snarled. I hit him with a right to the face, square on the nose, followed by a left to his midsection. He went down hard on his knees gushing blood and holding his face, then vomiting up the booze and the greasy digestion of a recent meal."

"His goon was a big ugly guy that looked like he had taken a few too many hits to the head with his damaged nose and scares around the eyes. The guy took a wild swing that I blocked. After a hard blow to his chin connected solidly, I battered him with repeated jabs to the face. He went down cold with blood flowing from his badly broken nose. Because I was enraged, I kicked the alderman in the jaw knocking him unconscious also."

Elliot paused a moment to let the emotion of the memory subside. "To shorten the rest of the story, I took Francis back to my place. She was frightened for her life. Rightly so, since this alderman was well connected with both police and organized crime. A couple of hours later, Eleanor shows up. She has a key to my flat and walks in and sees Francis in my bed. There's an ugly scene with her anger at what she thinks is going on, and my indignation at being falsely accused. Lots of shouting. Lots of things said by both of us that are tough to forget. It's never reconciled. Probably both our egos. At any rate, our relationship ends."

"Did you ever see her again?" Allison asks.

"No."

Elliot suggested it was time for lunch. They drove into Châteauneuf-du-Pape and settled in a small café off the main street.

He ordered a bottle of the excellent local wine while he interpreted the menu for Allison.

"And your father? What became of him?" Allison asked.

Elliot reflected for a few moments and his eyes teared slightly. "After I returned from Cuba, my father took ill and had to quit the mines. Like most miners he had black lung. I brought him to New York and he lived with me for two years before he died. He was only fifty. I grieved deeply. I loved that man who was a giant of a father as well as a mother to me. It was an enormous act of love that he sacrificed so much so that I would not face a life in the mines."

Allison was finding herself immersed progressively deeper into Elliot's story. He was truly *reliving* these events, or thought he was. If she didn't think about the chronology it was easy to accept Elliot's version of these events as real.

Lunch arrived. Elliot delighted in Allison's obvious savoring of her *bouillabaisse*, the signature Provencal fish soup. Elliot was a frequent customer and the owner made a fuss over Allison. She was sure to be the talk of the town with everyone wondering about the beautiful young woman visiting Monsieur Gaston.

Declining dessert but taking a few cheeses and coffee, Allison said, "Go on with your story, Elliot."

"Well. I prospered as a journalist. With a better offer, I went over to the *New York Times*. I was becoming a scourge to the politically corrupt. I elevated my targets from the street level low-lifes to the real bosses. There were times that I made my editor and even the publisher nervous. To their credit, they resisted a lot of political pressure. I had articles published in McClure's, kind of the exposé magazine of the times. You can check that out, Allison. Byline was *Dillan Murphy*."

"Wasn't that dangerous during those times?" Allison asked.

"Yes it was dangerous. But I was full of myself. Not stupid about what I was doing, but not fully realizing what the bad guys might try to do to quiet me. I took basic precautions; no walking down dark streets, always checking out those in my vicinity. What military types call situational awareness. But there was one time. A time that still haunts me."

Elliot continued. "I was at a bar with a friend, T.E. Fitzgerald's on Sixth Avenue and West Forty-Fourth. He was a young civil engineer working for the Interborough Rapid Transit Company, the subway company. Bright guy. He was destined for a great career with the success of the new subway system that had opened just a couple of years earlier. Quiet. Soft-spoken. Loved classical music. Got me interested in fine music. Anyway, we were having a couple of drinks in a bar. He was telling me about his recent engagement to a secretary at the IRT. Two guys came in. Tough looking guys with overcoats. My instincts perked as they clearly were looking around for someone. I grabbed Bill, my friend William Flynn, and pulled him out of his chair toward the back of the bar toward a rear door. I wasn't quick enough though. Bill took two bullets in the back meant for me. I would have been killed too except the bartender shot one guy with a sawed-off shotgun he kept behind the bar, then the other guy took off."

Elliot stopped his narrative and finished his coffee.

Allison interrupted the silence after a few moments, "Well?"

"Nothing more to say. I felt guilty, but didn't know how deeply until at the funeral his fiancé accused me of causing his death, then slapped my face. The experience of Bill Flynn's murder changed me. Hard to explain how, but I saw the world with a different perspective after that. I was no longer as arrogant. I couldn't manipulate everything around me. The world was no longer something to be conquered."

"That was an event that certainly had a profound impact on my life, but from there I'd like to skip ahead a bit. With my long history, I could go on for weeks. I want you to understand my life, and I want you to believe me, Allison. Do you?"

Allison looked down and responded, "I don't know, Elliot. I can feel it's so real when you're telling me about the past, but it's just so preposterous --- just so --- I just don't know, Elliot."

"That's ok. How about we go back to the house. I want to tell you about my experience in World War

One," Elliot said. "Of all things in my life, those experiences of perhaps a little more than a year had the most telling impact on my core beliefs."

The autumn day had turned cold. There was a hint of the Mistral, the cold, dry winter winds that blow across Provence from the north. Back at the house, Elliot started a fire in the hearth and set coffee to brewing. Allison joined him in the kitchen. They chatted about life in Provence; its unique culture, its cuisine, its love of wine, its celebration of life.

"Everything about this house is old, and well-used, yet it has an elegance that is difficult to describe. I guess this is the difference between *character* and interior design," Allison said.

"I guess that's what attracts me to Europe. The architecture and the rhythms of life are chronologically old, yet ageless. This house has permanence, almost its own personality. I feel part of this place," he said.

They adjourned to the living area with their coffees and a good bottle of Sauternes. "Now I shall tell you what at the time was called the Great War. It was a war fought with nineteenth century tactics and twentieth century weapons. It turned out to be a monumental stupid contest of politicians and generals. The carnage cannot be comprehended by later generations, only by those that experienced it," Elliot said.

"Your novel, *Ypres,* was extraordinarily evocative. It continues to be critically acclaimed. I thought it even better than Sebastian Faulks' *Birdsong* which came out a few years later," Allison said referring to his novel of World War I set in the Belgian battlefields of Flanders.

"Evocative? Such a literary word. But *Ypres* was still just a story. I want you to read my first novel, *Living Dead*, written in 1924. *Ypres* is more a literary work and better crafted, *Living Dead* is raw, more journalistic. I was attempting to capture in words the World War One experience in the trenches."

"I want to now recount to you some of my personal experiences, but these too will still just be words. The trenches in Flanders wrought another profound change in my life. My brief combat experience in Cuba could not begin to prepare me for this incarnation of hell," Elliot said.

Excerpt from *The Journal Of Dillan Murphy* – Flanders, Belgium - 1917

Although I had become a top reporter in New York with consistent front-page bylines, I was hungering to get my teeth into something different. Those early years of the new century were a time of turmoil throughout the world. There was the Boxer Rebellion in China where radicals attempted to drive out foreigners. There was the Boer War in what today is South Africa. There was a war between Russia and Japan, followed by an aborted revolution in Russia in 1905. There were the horrors perpetrated in colonial Belgian Congo and the genocide of Armenia. There was a revolution in Mexico. Then of course there was the run-up to World War One in Europe.

The question of America's entry into the War dominated the day. When the United States formally entered the War in April of 1917, I convinced my senior editor to post me to France even before American forces disembarked for France.

The War was three years old. Germany's aggression westward across Belgium, thereby threatening Paris, had been stopped by the massive infusion of British armies. By 1917 the War had evolved into a stalemate of appalling attrition of men and materiel. Opposing armies of a million men faced off in elaborate arrays of defensive trenches and concrete fortifications. The chessboard exe-

cution of the war by the generals belied the virtual hell
for the soldiers in the trenches.

I arrived in Paris in April of 1917. It was a glorious
spring and Paris was still *Paris*. Except for an unusual
amount of uniformed men about the Champs-Elysées, it
was everything I had read about. Paris had a unique
rhythm that was only slightly altered by the war raging
less than one hundred miles to the northeast. There were
the beginnings of real food shortages, but generally, if
you had money there was plenty of food, wine, and of
course, plenty of women in the City of Light.

It was a good month before I was able to sort out how
and where I wanted to report on the war. I spent the time
probing and ingratiating myself with high-ranking officers, both to secure their assistance as well as to get information for my pieces back to the States. From the perspective of Paris, the War seemed somewhat removed,
yet it raged only 100 miles to the east. The numbers of
combatants and casualties were staggering, so much so
that they became an abstraction. From 1914 to 1918, over
one million men would fall as casualties in Flanders
alone. Numbers simply could not convey the enormity of
the conflict there. Nothing in history came close to its
scale.

I dined with French and British officers that dressed
in immaculate uniforms, often accompanied by well-
dressed women. The restaurants had no shortages for
senior military officers. I suspected most had never even
been to the Front, much less experienced anything of the
kind of deprivations of the average soldier.

I will illustrate my point by way of an interesting personal footnote. One evening I was invited by a French
colonel to a private party held in a suite at the elegant
Hotel Meurice on the Rue de Rivoli. There were perhaps
a dozen men, all with young female escorts, myself included. Waiters served expensive wine and cigars on sil-

ver service. The entertainment for the evening was the notorious Mata Hari, the exotic courtesan and Oriental dancer. I learned later that she was actually Dutch. Her real name was Margaretha Zelle.

Mademoiselle Zelle put on quite a show. Although she was perhaps forty, she was still a great beauty. I don't know about her dancing talents, but her costume and provocative movements were enticing. She was dark as a gypsy. She was barefoot and sported an exotic looking beaded headdress. Over her breasts she wore a bra of two cup-like affairs with her midriff bare and a loose-fitting slit skirt riding low on her hips. The skirt looked to be of silk with elaborate embroidery. As she whirled about, her skirt periodically parted to reveal she had nothing on underneath. Toward the last of her performance she pulled off her skirt and danced nude with only her breasts covered. It was a gloriously decadent evening, one of the last before I went to the front.

To my dismay, I was to learn later that year that Mata Hari had been convicted by a French military court on charges of espionage for giving information to the Germans. By the newspaper accounts, the charges were ridiculous with no substantive evidence. War hysteria. An incompetent French General Staff perhaps looking to deflect their own failings. Hard to understand. Nevertheless, Mata Hari was executed by firing squad. The night that I saw her dance was perhaps her last performance. That evening seemed from another time after a few months at the Front in the trenches.

I attached myself to Major Crawford of the Irish Guards First Battalion of the British Expeditionary Force. He was no rear-echelon staff officer. To the contrary he was hell-bent to be right in the thick of the fight.

"I'm returning to my regiment in two days, Mister Murphy. If you wish to see what this war is really about, I shall take you up to the Front," Crawford said. "I've been in this fight since '14. Rough go back then. The Krauts almost pushed us back, but we held Flanders and therefore we held France. Now it's an ugly contest fought from muddy holes."

The British were the primary Allied forces fighting in Belgium. The bulk of the French forces were to the south. The United States had not yet entered the War in early 1917.

The Major and I rode in an ambulance eastward from the town of Poperinghe toward Ypres with the front lines just a few miles further east of the town. While still miles from the British lines, the terrain started to abruptly change. From functioning farms to damaged farms and barns, then to no structures, then to no trees, then to no grass. The once great town of Ypres with its grand Cloth Hall built in the thirteenth century and its imposing cathedral had been reduced to rubble by German artillery over the past years of constant fighting. Every building was destroyed or damaged. The civilian population had long since left.

A few miles beyond Ypres, the ambulance deposited us at a place where a large tent had been erected over an excavated area. The Major informed me this was the Regiment's headquarters, a couple of miles to the rear of the front line trenches.

Motioning to a soldier, the Major said to me, "This here's Staff Sergeant Gallagher. Follow his lead and you'll have as good a chance as any to survive. The Sergeant's a top soldier. Sergeant?"

"Sir!" the Sergeant braced to attention with the compliment. He looked like an old hand with a lean build that suggested a wirery strength, punctuated with a well-groomed large, red mustache.

"This is Mister Murphy, Sergeant. Newspaper correspondent from the States. He wants to go up to the front with us tomorrow. Give him what assistance you can."

The Major entered the tent and left me with the Sergeant.

The Sergeant offered his hand. "Glad to meet you, Sir. Are you Irish, Sir?"

"Irish descent. Both my mother and my father's parents came from Ireland," I answered.

"Well I'd say you're Irish then, Sir. We'll be relieving the Grenadier Guards Second Battalion who'll change places with us here in the rear. You see we've got two of the Brigade's battalions on the front line with two held in reserve. Theory is, if there's an attack, the reserve battalions can be directed to plug any breach in our lines," the Sergeant explained.

"Early call, Sir, three AM. I'll show you to a place where you can a get a wee bit of rest. Do ya have plenty of socks, Sir."

"I think so, but why's that so important?" I asked.

"Must keep your feet dry. You need to change at least three times a day otherwise you're apt to get trench foot. Trench foot is some mean shit, Sir. You'll want to be avoidin' it. I'll get you some extra from the quartermaster. Can't have too many socks."

I picked up my gear, which was typical conventional British Army issue. It was a heavy load totaling about fifty pounds consisting of a large backpack, haversack, blanket, ground sheet, water bottle, eating tin, shovel, helmet, and gas mask. In place of a rifle, I carried a portable Corona typewriter in a wooden case.

As we were walking, it started to rain so I broke out my waterproof cape. The Sergeant remarked, "Fuckin' rain, if you pardon my French. Freeze your arse off in the winter, then it rains almost every bloody day in the spring."

Sergeant Gallagher took me a short way to a ladder descending into a trench. He explained that though we were in the rear of the front lines, German artillery could reach this far, so even here they lived in trenches. It was to be my first taste of trench life.

The trench was about eight feet deep. Rainwater ran down the sides filling the bottom. There was a so-called trench board that you walked on that elevated you from the water depending upon the amount of rain. I followed the Sergeant into a large room-type excavation covered with a wooded roof. The bunker was crowded with soldiers who all looked toward us as we entered.

"This here's Mister Murphy. He's a newspaperman from America, but he's Irish. Goin' up to the line with us. He'll be making you famous back home 'less you'll be showin' him what a bunch of dumb shits you are," the Sergeant said.

The men were of good cheer and we shook hands all around. I unbuckled my gear and sat down on a long wooden bench. There were no bunks. At best I might find enough room to lie down on the wood planking. The floor was mud, getting worse as more rain water poured down the walls of the excavation. Sitting up, I dosed fitfully for a few hours until Sergeant Gallagher rattled a mess tin with his bayonet to rouse the platoon. It was the middle of the night.

I fell out with the rest of the soldiers. Everyone was silent and grim. They had done this before. The fellow next to me said it would take two hours to cover the two miles to the front trenches. "Why so long?" I asked.

"It's tough going. You'll see why in bit," he answered.

It was not long before the terrain began to change. Shell craters became increasing numerous until there was no direct route, only a serpentine traverse through a field of gaping holes filled with water. In places you sunk calf-deep into the mud. Only where there were wooden *duckboards* was it possible to walk normally.

"It's a good night to be on the march. Black as the Kaiser's soul," the soldier next to me whispered. "If they spot us, their artillery would do a bloody number on us out here in the open."

Sergeant Gallagher kicked the soldier in the butt and whispered. "Shut your mouth you stupid bugger. If the Jerries lob any artillery on us, I'll put a bullet through that empty head of yours."

We arrived at the beginning of the front trench fortifications as dawn was breaking. The trenches were not mere holes, but rather a complex network of parallel and perpendicular excavations designed to anchor a defensive position. In the coming days I would learn that there were front line and secondary line traverse trenches, connected by perpendicular service and communication trenches. Underground bunkers were periodically spaced to store supplies and afford some soldiers shelter from the elements.

Beyond the front lines was a surreal landscape starting with rows of barbed wire entanglements followed by ground so corrupted that the rims of shell craters literally joined each other. A few stumps of sheared-off trees jutted from the ground, otherwise the landscape was totally devoid of any vegetation. I glimpsed this through angled observation binoculars that allowed the viewer to stay below the trench rim. Exposing your head would invite a German sniper's bullet.

"Jesus, Sergeant, if that isn't a vision of Hell I don't know what is," I remarked as I surveyed the landscape through the glasses.

"Right you are, Sir. It is Hell," Sergeant Gallagher said. "When you're out there you have to give up any hope of surviving. Bullets zipping by. Artillery rounds and grenades sending terrible shrapnel about. There's the fucking gas, a stupid weapon, and ugly as sin. Then there're the machine guns. Take out a whole platoon in a couple of minutes, they can. Seen it happen. All this as you're stumbling through this artillery plowed field and the endless mud. Seen many a soldier drown in a crater hole filled with water. Or you might just sink out of sight in some mud holes that are like quicksand. Better to die by a bullet I say."

"How long have you been here Sergeant?" I asked.

"Since '15. Survived Loos and the Somme. Not many of us original regulars left. All these lads about you are fresh enlistees or conscripts. Good lads, but still don't have the training."

"How often do you attack?" I asked.

"Every time General Haig has a fart caught crosswise and thinks it's an original thought. Bloody too often if you ask me. And you know what happens if you're lucky enough to make it across no-man's land without being hit? You get to occupy the German's trenches. This shithole we're in right now used to be German trenches we took from them a year ago. That's all there is here in Flanders, endless trenches. Just trade one hole for another, but only after you kill thousands on both sides."

It started to rain. "Fucking rain. That's all it's done since the start of spring. Newbury, front and center," the Sergeant said, signaling a soldier.

"Newbury, this is Mister Murphy, newspaper man from America. Be a good lad and help him get about."

"Peter Newbury. Pleased to meet you, Mister Murphy," the Private said and shook hands. He was a big-eared kid with a big grin. "Grab your gear and we'll find a place for ya in the bunker."

I started to question the wisdom of wanting to be up here on the front lines as we sloshed down the trench. Boards lined the bottom of the trench so you could walk without sinking, but the water was still over the boards and up to your ankles. I could see why the extra socks. If the rain persisted, you were going to stand in water a good deal of the day.

By a *place*, Private Newbury meant a spot not otherwise occupied. There were no bunks, no chairs, no tables. I put my waterproof ground sheet down and parked my gear. The bunker itself was a depressing place, just a wider hole than the trenches with a leaking wooden roof and duckboard floor, lit by some kerosene lamps. It smelled of damp unwashed bodies.

Most of the men of the Second Platoon of Company A were in their teens or early twenties. I couldn't imagine a crueler place, yet they were of surprisingly high spirits. In spite of being forced to live worse than an animal, with the strong likelihood of death or wounding that awaited their future, they joked and generally took care of each other. I believed it was a means to hold their individual terrors in check.

I intended to write about these brave men, to put a human face to this terrible conflict for my readers back in the States. By all indications, the United States would soon be entering the conflict. Americans needed to see beyond the lofty patriotic soundings by public figures and understand what it would mean to their young men. This was not to be a war of quick adventure like the Spanish-American War.

After an evening of playing cards, smoking, and finishing off their daily rum ration, those not on guard duty found their spots to sleep for the night. I too wrapped myself with my blanket and attempted to try to sleep. It was not to be. The rain persisted with an even heavier downpour. Water flowed down the walls of the bunker raising the ground water level well above the duckboard floor. Everyone sought a way to not have to sit or lay in the water. The best I could do was lean against the sloping bunker wall with my feet in the rising water.

Bad as this was, there was worse. Once the lamps were extinguished I could hear noises of what sounded like the scurrying of small animals. Something touched my thigh. "Newbury? What's that noise?" I asked urgently in a harsh whisper.

"Rats. Big fuckin' rats. Won't bother you though. They're just scavenging for food. Everything always needs to be secured in crates or the bastards will get into the rations."

I willed myself to suppress the panic, then lit a match. Staring up between my feet was the ugliest looking rat I had ever seen, literally the size of a rabbit. "Sonofabitch!" I yelled and dropped the match. "Christ, did you see the size of that rat, Newbury?"

"Seen bigger I'm afraid. We call 'em corpse rats. They been feedin' off corpses. You see, there's a whole lot of dead out there from both sides that never got a proper burial. Lots of bodies you can't get to after a battle. Lots just sink into the mud. Everything freezes over in the winter, then come spring they start popping up. Rats have a feast."

"Wonderful. So what do you do about them?" I asked.

"Nothing you can do. They won't bite you. Some blokes kill 'em for sport. Some have been known to eat them. Meat rations are rare. As for me, no thanks. Not eatin' rat that's been feeding on a rottin' corpse," Newbury said.

The bile rose in my throat. Needless to say, my first night in the front line trenches was sleepless.

As daylight broke, there were groans and curses as the platoon woke. Breakfast was a small ration of soggy bread, a bit of cheese, and a tin of tepid tea. The rain persisted in a steady downpour. I ventured outside the bunker with my rain cape and explored up and down the trench. Apart from the sentries stationed every twenty yards, the rest of the men did the best they could to keep dry. As I passed, gaunt unshaved faces looked out from boltholes every few steps along the trench. Boltholes were simply dugout areas in the wall of the trenches large enough for a man to squirrel himself into. It was a little drier there and some added protection against shrapnel from aerial artillery bursts.

With a horrid night spent with the rats and the privations of the soldiers I saw that first day, it took all my will to muster the courage to stay on out there. This was something out of medieval history. But I stuck it out. The day proved productive as I saw the battlefield from the Soldier's eye.

I didn't relish nighttime, but knowledge is better than the unknown. I was exhausted and dosed only fitfully that second night. It was a short night. Around three in the morning the German shelling started. There is simply no way to adequately describe the terror of an artillery bombardment.

First of all there is nowhere to hide. My first instinct was to get out of the bunker. Its low roof made me claustrophobic. The unrelenting noise and the uncertainty if the round was going to land near could reduce even the strongest willed to paralysis. Close explosions hurt your ears and showered debris.

I was huddled with a couple of soldiers sitting on the firing platform of the trench. No more than thirty feet away, a shell exploded directly within the trench, the concussion of its explosion knocking all of us into the water at the trench bottom. I didn't feel that I had been wounded, but my front was covered with blood and pieces of tissue. The soldier next to me screamed and fought frantically to dislodge the severed hand in his lap.

The bombardment kept up for four hours. The noise was virtually constant only increasing in magnitude when rounds exploded close by. Conversation was impossible even if anybody wanted to say anything. At seven o'clock, the bombardment abruptly ceased.

I made my way to the young platoon lieutenant looking into no-man's land with the observation glasses. "Sergeant Gallagher, get the platoon into firing position and fix bayonets," he shouted.

The rain had ceased but it was still a deeply overcast morning with a heavy fog hugging the ground. "Lieutenant, are you expecting an attack?" I asked.

"No question about it. That bombardment was across a several mile front. Anytime now. We'll first hear firing from our forward observers, then they'll pull back to this line. Then our own batteries will open up on the Germans. I must tell you Mister Murphy, that if the Jerries get into our trenches they'll take you for a soldier. You being without a weapon won't stop them from killing you or taking you prisoner. I suggest you stay close to the Sergeant, Sir."

I thanked the Lieutenant and went to prepare my gear in the event that we retreated. I also pulled out a Colt M1911 .45 caliber semi-automatic in a leather shoulder holster. A friend from my Rough Rider days was still in the U.S. Army. I kept in contact and upon learning that I was going to France, he suggested I take along the U.S. Army officer's newest sidearm. I was officially a non-combatant but that distinction is lost on an enemy soldier faced with someone in the uniform of the other side.

I found myself next to Private Newbury. "What's going to happen, Peter? Have you been under attack before?" I asked.

"Many a time."

"Ever have to retreat?"

"Aye. Been in two retreats. But I tell you, Mister Murphy, defendin's a damn site better than doin' the attacking," Newbury said. "When you're to go over the top, the fear's enough to cause you to mess yourself. Bet-

ter to be in the hole and have the other feller be runin'
about ducking bullets while crawlin' through barbed
wire. And if you're wounded out there, well you're all
but fucked."

Made sense, but I can bear witness that defending
was little better. Within minutes, British artillery batteries
commenced their own barrage against the advancing
German forces, although the fog prevented sighting the
enemy. Soon, machine guns opened up. Put enough bullets out there and you'll hit some of the enemy. I guessed
that the advancing Germans were visible as the entire
platoon opened up with their Lee Enfield rifles.

For the next thirty minutes the fighting raged with
the Brits firing and reloading as rapidly as possible. Then
the first grenade came into the trench. A soldier standing
next to me took the grenade's shrapnel and saved me.
Then I heard other grenades exploding in the trenches. It
meant that the Germans were gaining ground. Within
minutes our section of trench turned to confusion.

Sergeant Gallagher was rallying his men. The Lieutenant had been killed. Gallagher sent a runner to the left
to see what the Company's orders were. One soldier
looked pleadingly to Gallagher. "Sarge, we're bein' overrun. We've got to retreat!"

"Shut your fuckin' face, Soldier. We'll hold until I get
orders otherwise."

Moments later, the runner returned. "Sergeant, the
Captain says pull back to the secondary trenches and
consolidate defenses."

"Retreat! Retreat!" Gallagher yelled. At the same
time, men came running down the trench from the right
only to be cut down by Germans firing from behind
them. The Germans had apparently overrun that portion
of the trench. Several men fell from their standing firing
positions and a German soldier jumped into the trench
twenty feet from me. With no hesitation, I unholstered

my .45 and shot him twice in the chest before he could discharge his Mauser. I grabbed by typewriter and journals and ran as best as I could through the standing water down the communication trench toward the rear trench line.

After a hundred yards I reached the secondary defensive trench, only to find that the entire Corps was falling back across a broad front. That meant leaving the relative protection of the trenches to navigate the crater-pocked landscape, hoping not to be blown up by artillery, or drowned in the mud. This was the same ground the Platoon covered the day before.

The German artillery started to land rounds into the rear of our lines to inflict casualties on the retreating forces. So the further you got from the front trenches, the worse it became. With every shell-burst men fell. Instinct wanted to force you to seek cover. I clearly expected not to escape the artillery. The terror compelled me to slide down the side of a large shell crater filled with water to at least gain some moments of rest.

Within moments I regretted the move. As I slid down the side of the hole into the water, I collided with something. Fortunately there was only three feet of water in this shell hole. Turning to see what I had struck, I recoiled at the sight of the upper torso of a soldier. It was badly decomposed. The face was gone. It was disgusting beyond all description. A recent artillery shell had probably dislodged it. But to consummate my horror, a large rat emerged from the abdominal cavity, offal caked about its snout.

Retching, I scrambled out of the crater like a madman.

Hours later I reached the new defensive trench line. I was given a blanket and a ration of rum, then fell asleep until the next dawn. After considerable searching, I found the Second Platoon, or what was left of it. Sergeant

Gallagher, Private Newbury, and eight others were all that remained of the fifty-seven men the day before.

I slapped Private Newbury on the back. "Peter, it's good to see you."

Newbury barely acknowledged my presence. Both he and Sergeant Gallagher had the *thousand-yard stare* of those that had been pushed to the limits of emotionally being able to function. "Sergeant, I'm glad you made it. Seems you have nine lives," I said.

"More than nine. Should have died more times than I could count. God is just being cruel. He lets me see all these young lads torn apart, then spares me to repeat it over and over. In the end, in the last battle, He will have me butchered too."

I cannot fully explain why I stayed out there in the trenches with the British soldiers rather than file my stories with headquarter interviews, and billet myself somewhere with at least minimal necessities. But I felt that this was a unique opportunity to experience something profound. These were events never to be repeated. As much as I wanted safety and basic creature comforts, I felt I would be betraying myself if I cut and ran this early on.

Only the numbing fear of battle distracts the poor bastard in the trench from dealing with the filth and deprivations. Over the next couple of weeks I lived in conditions worse than subhuman. The rain never relented. Keeping dry was impossible. When the rain did stop, mud caked your clothing. Even without the rain, there was standing water in all the trenches due to the boggy terrain around Ypres, so keeping your feet dry was a constant endeavor. And the water itself was beyond disgust. Stagnant, full of urine, sometimes things worse than that, frequently populated with ugly fat slugs and a scum of algae.

I saw men with trench foot, their feet swollen and deformed to twice normal size. At best it was excruciatingly painful, at worse the feet were amputated. It is such a disgusting affliction that once when doing a piece about a field hospital, I had to go outside to vomit.

Fierce looking beetles crawled in the boltholes feeding on the body lice infestations breeding where the men would sleep. With no means of washing bodies or clothing, body lice was a chronic condition with every soldier. They fed on blood, creating a nasty, itching rash around your waist, underarms, and around your groin area.

Decomposing corpses, both human and horse, open latrines, and unwashed bodies fueled a pervasive stench. There were no trees, no grass. Often there was no sky. There were no birds, no rabbits, no squirrels. The only living creatures were all manner of disgusting vermin, and men.

The British Army regrouped. A new Second Platoon was formed with survivors of other units. We counterattacked two weeks later.

··········

Elliot paused his story and seemed lost for a moment in the memories.

Allison had sat silently absorbed through Elliot's long narrative. At his obvious break she said, "My God, Elliot. I read much of this in your novel *Yres*, but hearing your own personal experience is emotionally jarring. You make my skin crawl with your descriptions."

"Probably was a bad place to break since we should be thinking about dinner," Elliot said.

"Dinner? After talk of rats and lice? Besides, I had a large lunch. Maybe something light later?" Allison suggested.

"Sounds good to me. Perhaps some cheese and bread when we get hungry. How about more wine though?" Elliot asked.

"Sure. You do like your wine, don't you?"

"Wine is such a sublime pleasure, it can never be considered a vice. I'm going to open a Bordeaux. Actually I prefer Bordeaux to the Rhone wines from here, but I do my best to exhibit local loyalty," Elliot said, then went to fetch a bottle from the cellar. Returning, he commented, "One of my favorites. Left bank of the river that divides the Bordeaux region, heavier on the Cabernet than the softer, less tannic Merlot based Bordeaux of the right bank. Love 'em both actually."

He opened the bottle and poured the wine into a decanter. "Adds air and helps to release the bouquet. Actually you should decant it a couple of hours before drinking, but we'll just have to rough it."

He poured two glasses and settled back into his chair. "Back to the Great War."

Excerpt from *The Journal Of Dillan Murphy* – Flanders, Belgium - 1917

Just like the German's, the British batteries delivered a several hour barrage. Once the infantry moved forward, the barrage was maintained progressively preceding the British advance to disrupt the Germans from consolidating an effective defense.

I followed slightly in to the rear with the medical and supply personnel. By the end of the day the Irish Guards occupied the same trenches that they had been driven out of two weeks previously. The exchange of these few thousand yards of real estate came at a cost of many thousands of casualties on both sides.

I again linked up with Sergeant Gallagher and the Second Platoon. Private Newbury had survived the assault, but clearly he had changed. Another private sitting next to Newbury said to me, "Peter'll be all right once we're relieved up here. Word has it we're due any time now. Just hope that Haig or Gough doesn't get ambitious with our lives," the soldier said referring to the two commanding British generals. "How the fuck does someone make general being so bloody fuckin' stupid? They just keep killing us then replacing the numbers with new boys from home. Soon there won't be any fellows left in Ireland or England."

The soldier nudged Newbury, "Peter. Ya know what I think? If we're to be surviving this war, there'll be a hell of lot more girls to go around. Could be we'll be in high demand. Could ya do with a fine piece of ass, Peter? Ah, I can smell that fine smell now."

Newbury made no response, only barely registering that he had even heard.

I asked the soldier, "You're Irish. Why are you here fighting for the British? Did you enlist or were you conscripted?"

"Well, it seemed like a good thing at the time. Don't hate the British like some Irish do. All that rubbish is old history. Seemed to me that the Germans would own the Continent if they weren't stopped. That happened, Ireland and England are in some deep shit. German's are a warlike bunch of fuckers, ya know. Besides, my prospects were poor and the Army seemed like the best thing at the time. Didn't know about this fucking trench warfare though. Rather be scroungin' for a meal in Dublin right now than out here in this muddy hole."

"We'll, that's well put, Private. I could not have stated my thoughts anymore concisely, and I'm a writer. I'll use your insights in my next dispatch back to the States," I said.

Actually I probably would not. My editor back at the *New York Times* admonished me for the slant to my recent copy. His words: 'too personal. You depict the horrors of the War admirably, but frankly they're a little lurid. I think our readers are looking for more balance that illustrates the larger strategic struggle. A struggle that will inevitably bring the United States into the War, with young Americans called upon to fight Germany. Need more uplifting reporting and details on the Allies' progress. What about a piece that shows America's contribution to arming and supplying the British and France?'

Utter bullshit from a self-serving asshole was my reaction. Rumor was that he intended to run for national office.

Unfortunately for the Platoon, rotation to the rear did not come before the unit was called on to resume the assault within two days. It's truly a frightful thing to wait before going over the top of the trench into the teeth of enemy fire. This time it would be worse. Because of the terrain with its shallow groundwater, the German Fourth Army had established a strong defensive line using concrete pillboxes, situated to provide an interlocking field of fire from machine guns.

British high command wanted to exploit their counter-offensive. After a couple of days for regrouping and re-supply, General Gough meant to try to dislodge the Germans from their reinforced defensive line. The British artillery barrage commenced at three o'clock in the morning. The men assembled at the edge of the trench. Sergeant Gallagher called out down the line, "Time for makin' ready lads. Fix your bayonets."

No man spoke. All were consumed with their own thoughts. They all knew that unlike the attack that had just pushed back the German's, this one was going to be tougher, and bloodier. One man was shaking badly. Several appeared to be praying. One obviously had wet himself as a large stain spread down his leg. Private Newbury looked disoriented.

Minutes later the barrage stopped and whistles sounded up and down the line as officers signaled the men to leave the trenches and move forward. Newbury did not climb up. Instead, he turned and sat down.

The Lieutenant screamed at him from atop the trench, "Newbury, you get your fuckin' bloody arse movin' or I'll have you shot!"

Newbury did not budge, just stared into nowhere. The Lieutenant jumped back down into the trench. He came up to Newbury and pointed his Webley revolver at Newbury's head. "Last time I'll be tellin' you, Newbury."

The Lieutenant looked over at me apparently deciding not to shoot Newbury right there. "Mister Murphy, you're a witness to this cowardice. I will have you stand to a firing squad, Newbury." With that, the Lieutenant climbed out of the trench to join his Platoon.

Through the observation glasses I watch the British forces advance on the German line. The lightly defended forward German positions were quickly overtaken. Once within range of the concrete machinegun emplacements however, the Irish Guards fell in increasing numbers. There was seemingly a point beyond which they could not advance as the dead and dying mounted under the withering fire. The attack seemed completely pointless. Forty minutes later, the remains of the Second Platoon stumbled back into the trench around me.

Sergeant Gallagher was among the survivors. After barking orders to attend to his wounded, he came and sat next to me. "Seems I've survived another battle. I lost men today that I didn't even know what their names were. This is absolute madness. I will go on until I am killed. So will every man here. The war ended a long time ago with this idiotic stalemate, but the slaughter still goes on. This is now a place where men only die. Only the politicians and generals continue to talk about victory."

Several men were wounded, some badly. The Lieutenant was among those walking wounded with his left arm hanging limply and dripping blood. His face was contorted in rage as he walked down the trench. "Sergeant, come with me and find Private Newbury."

I followed them the short distance to a dugout hole where Newbury sat staring blankly.

"On your feet, Private!" the Lieutenant shouted. Sergeant Gallagher grabbed Newbury by one arm and forced him to his feet. "Sergeant, arrest this man for cowardice in the face of the enemy and desertion. He refused my order to advance with the rest of the Platoon. He stayed behind like a sniveling coward while good men died in his stead. You'll be tried and shot, Newbury. See that he gets to the rear under guard, Sergeant."

Was Newbury a coward? Were the guys that shook uncontrollably, that pissed themselves, braver because they still went out to die? Newbury had fought a good deal before this latest incident. Was this a conscious act on his part, or did he just emotionally shut down? In this crucible of horror nothing was that simple.

Three weeks later, I attended Private Newbury's court marshal. The details of the trial are not important, and they weren't to the panel of British officers trying Newbury. He was defended, if it could be called that, by a young infantry lieutenant with no legal training. His cross-examination of Newbury's commanding lieutenant and one other soldier only made the prosecution's allegations stronger. The whole sham lasted thirty minutes. Found guilty of desertion in the face of the enemy, the presiding trial officer sentenced Newbury to death by firing squad. The sentence was to be carried out three weeks hence pending concurrence by the Commanding General.

I was allowed access to Newbury. He was held in a warehouse to the rear of the front lines in the city of Poperinge. There were a dozen prisoners held there in this makeshift jail.

"How are you fairing, Peter," I asked Newbury. "Do you need anything?"

Newbury barely acknowledged my presence. Still with that vacant stare he said, "I'm fine. Got my cigarettes. They give me all I want. Guess that's because they're going to shoot me."

"Tell me why you refused to follow your unit that day, Peter. Didn't you know what would happen?"

"Don't know. Just couldn't. Don't remember much about that day really. Do the other fellows in the Platoon think I'm a coward?" he asked.

"No, they don't think you're a coward. They feel badly about your – your circumstance," I said. The truth was that those survivors of the disastrous attack had mixed feelings about Private Newbury's refusal. Characterizing the pervasive fatalism, one soldier simply said, 'Doesn't matter much, but the bloke should of gone over the top and died out there. We're all goin' to die anyway."

With some pull from Major Crawford the Chief of Staff for the Irish Guards who took me to the Front, I was allowed to attend the execution.

At 6:00 AM on a gray day with a slight drizzle of rain, Private Peter Newbury was marched outside. I was impressed with his composure as he was tied to a stake in front of the brick warehouse wall. A priest spoke to him and Newbury shook his head. I assumed this was in response to the offer of a last statement. The priest touched him on the face with the sign of the cross then backed away. An officer placed a black hood over Newbury's head. A medical officer pinned a white piece of cloth over his heart to act as a target.

Before the volley of fire that extinguished his life, I could see the hood over Newbury's head sucking in and out as his final anxiety made him gulp for breath.

Newbury's execution was not an isolated event. After the war I learned that the British executed over 300 soldiers for desertion or cowardice.

■ ■ ■ ■ ■ ■ ■ ■ ■ ■

Allison sat transfixed as Elliot paused his story. "My God. Along with listening, I've been watching you tell me this story. You've been almost physically reliving that experience," she said.

"Whenever I think of that time, I can't quite put it into a category. It transcends logic. Words always seem to fall short. It was a war like no other. Nothing I've ever read adequately explains why this mass killing of young men went on for so long when for the last two years of the conflict there was no chance of anything approximating victory for either side. Every general and political leader had to know that at best they might only effect a better position from which to bargain armistice terms. For this, millions died. Instead of the Newburys, those that perpetuated the War should have been shot. My experiences left me with an abiding cynicism about governments, and a hatred for nationalism."

Elliot continued. "Ah, it's late and we haven't had dinner. I'll fix us something simple if that's ok?"

He fixed a salad of tomatoes and fresh mozzarella cheese covered with a liberal serving of an excellent, light olive oil. Some cold ham with bread made a respectable light meal.

While they ate, Allison asked, "And after that episode with the soldier's execution, what happened?"

"There was much more to my World War One experience, but let me shorten that part of my tale. I spent the rest of 1917 with the British troops. I witnessed the terrible carnage at Passenchendaele in Flanders. In a span of a few weeks, over a quarter of a million men fell there. It was worse carnage then the events I just recounted but my sensibilities had become numbed. My stories lost their personal elements, becoming just dull statistical reports. An angry editor had me transferred south to report on the American Expeditionary Force as it entered the conflict."

Elliot continued. "This relentless killing of tens of thousands of men had warped the world. After accompanying the American forces at the battle of St. Mihiel in September, 1918, I had had enough. The *Times* was unhappy with my copy. My copy was either dull or inflammatory. They cited the recently passed espionage acts that prohibited not only criticism of the War, but criticism of even the Government of the United States. So much for the sacred First Amendment. As for me, I was sick of the *Times* editorial demands and censorship. So I quit."

"So how old were you in 1918?" Allison asked.

"I would have been forty-five. Probably looked no more than thirty," Elliot answered.

"Then what?"

"I was disillusioned with American war propaganda and censorship. Obviously it was no place to express free intellectual thought at that time. So I went to Paris. Amazingly, Paris seemed outwardly unchanged by the years of war. After the Armistice, the shortages of the War disappeared almost immediately. People were intoxicated with the end of the War. Women were plentiful and exuberant. I should probably have felt guilty for taking advantages of the situation during that atmosphere. Young men were scarce. All able bodied Frenchmen had been conscripted and their numbers decimated with the carnage of four years of war. The streets of Paris were testimony to how much the War had reduced the population of France's manhood."

Elliot related how he decided to stay in Paris. He now spoke French. New York had no calling since he had quit the newspaper. There was no family. He had a modest amount of money saved. An American could live relatively inexpensively in Paris after the War because of the exchange rate. Now was a perfect time to try writing and decompress from the experiences of the last two years.

He took up residence in a small fourth story flat on Rue Clément. A dormer window provided a rooftop view of the Left Bank and the towers of St. Sulpice church. There was enough light to feel comfortable writing there, although he did spend a considerable amount of time writing at the cafes.

"For several years I attacked writing with an intense energy. Since I wrote in English, I was fortunate enough to get a couple of short stories published in England and the United States. Not much in the way of money, but it did establish modest creative writing credentials," Elliot said.

"What were the stories about, Elliot?" Allison asked.

"A couple about the War. One essay about the similarities and contrasts of New York and Paris. Of course I was working on my novel, *Living Dead*," Elliot answered.

Elliot told her that he never felt freer. None of the drudgery of his former journalistic career. He could now tell his own stories rather than the stories and the lies of others. No more deadlines, no more contesting with editors. Elliot described how he fell in with the expatriate American literary community and came to know some of the great writers of our time.

"You mean you knew Hemmingway, Scott Fitzgerald, Ezra Pound? And you frequented Gertrude Stein's salon?" Allison asked.

"Yes. Stein's house was on Rue de Fleurus. Actually I didn't hang out there like some. Hard to understand when some of them did any work, and how they could work with as much drinking that went on. But it certainly was a stimulating intellectual environment. I was more like Hemmingway in my work habits. I disciplined myself to write every day as he said he did."

"What was Hemmingway like?" Allison asked.

"We'll we weren't real pals. Casual friends maybe. We shared the common experience of being in the War. He clearly was more enthralled with the glory and adventure of war than I was. He was a big roaring bull of man, a lot like TR. Always doing larger than life masculine adventures. He wasn't as arrogant and full of himself as he became later on. Hell of a writer though. I loved his writing. His terse journalistic-styled prose. Guess most everyone did. But to your question, I'll tell you about one time I spent a week with him in Spain."

"My God, you knew Hemmingway that well? When was this?" Allison asked barely able to conceal her enthusiasm.

"1924. Hemmingway was a bullfighting enthusiast, as everyone knows. To him, the contest of the matador with the bull transcended the spectacle and even the danger aspects. It was an art form with metaphysical overtones. His wife Hadley chose to stay in Sevilla with friends while he and I journeyed to the town of Ronda, situated on this spectacular gorge in the hills of Andalusia. The journey was partly to see Ronda's magnificent Plaza de Toros bullring, partly to do some serious drinking."

Elliot continued. "But Hemmingway experienced something more profound in Ronda than bullfighting. You see Spain was different than the rest of Europe at that time. Economically and socially it suffered arrested development. Its poor were more impoverished than any other country in Western Europe. Corruption dominated all public institutions. The peasants were brutalized under almost medieval circumstances."

"Southern Spain, the Andalusia, was as bad as any area. Between our drinking adventures, we ventured out into the countryside and interacted with the people. Their miserable circumstances profoundly affected him. That earlier experience in the twenties drew him back in the late thirties to cover the Spanish Civil War as a journalist. His reporting was one-sided, always favoring the political leftist Popular Front."

Elliot and Allison chatted for sometime about his personal experiences with some of the greatest writers of the century. Elliot was expansive on everything except his personal life, particularly as it came to women.

"Elliot, you sound like a journalist. You're not telling me about your own life. You started to imply that there were lots of women in Paris in the twenties, but you never go beyond that. So what about your love life? You did have one I assume?"

Elliot smiled. "Oh yes. An active love life, or at least sex life. On reflection, I guess I feel a little guilty about all my conquests. A continuation of my misspent youth in New York. The roaring twenties is an apt name for the times. Women were forging new lifestyles and freedoms. Sex was part of that change. Paris was in the vanguard. I didn't usually spend nights alone unless I chose it that way."

"What kind of women were they?" Allison asked.

"All types. They worked in shops. There was a teacher, a violinist, a journalist. Most were strong-willed. All were intelligent. I learned to appreciate a wide range of new things. On the subject of sex, I was taught new things there as well. The French were clearly not as repressed in sexual expression as Americans. I wasn't exactly new to sexual experiences, but I was taught more than a thing or two, particularly how to pleasure them.

Maybe because I gravitated to the type, but these women were often assertive in bed. Obviously, most of them were not virgins."

"My, my. Now that's what I want to hear more about, Elliot," Allison said.

"Well I don't want you to think I was just a sexual adventurer. Among those Paris girls I met my future wife. Her name was Dominique. She was a student at the Sorbonne," Elliot said. "Studying chemistry of all things I was to learn,"

"What was she like? How did you meet?" Allison asked. Her eyes had been growing sleepy, but now were bright and attentive.

Excerpt from *The Journal Of Dillan Murphy* **– Paris, France - 1925**

I met Dominique Bellamont at an outdoor café on the Rue du Vieux Colombier. It was May, 1925. A sunny, warm day, late in the afternoon. This beautiful young woman sat down at the table next to me. She was tall, wore no makeup, and was dressed like a shop girl in a white blouse and gray skirt. She carried a canvas satchel that appeared fairly heavy.

The waiter approached her. "Mademoiselle?"

"Coffee, please."

"Something to eat, Mademoiselle?"

She hesitated before answering, "I think not."

In watching her I got the feeling that she perhaps was budgeting her money. I wanted to offer to buy her something but knew she would not accept. Then an elderly woman walking a large dog passed by on the sidewalk. The dog ducked under the young woman's table, wrapping the leash around the base. In trying to extricate itself, the dog tilted the table, spilling the woman's coffee and dropping the satchel, spilling books and papers.

I went to the aid of both women immediately, untangling the dog's leash to the thanks of the elderly woman who pulled her dog away and left hurriedly. The young woman and I bent down to pick up her books while I went about gathering her papers, which had blown about.

"*Merci beaucoup, Monsieur*," the young woman said.

"My pleasure, Mademoiselle," I said in English and offered my hand. "My name is Dillan Murphy."

She took my hand and replied in English, "My name is Dominique Bellamont."

I motioned to a waiter, and ordered another coffee for both of us. "Perhaps a menu also, Garcon."

"I find I am a little hungry. Would you join me?"

"Thank you, but you have already been too kind, Monsieur."

"But I would consider it a real pleasure, Mademoiselle Ballamont." She was hungry and apparently not offended by me, so she accepted and I joined her table.

She instantly struck me. Her eyes spoke of intelligence. Her hair was long, but pinned up in careless fashion with errant strands falling over her ears. She was tall with an excellent figure. Women's apparel of the time consisted of ground-length skirts and neck-high blouses, showing no flesh, but were at least form fitting. One could accurately assess the size of breasts and the slimness of waist. Apart from these noticeable assets, Mme. Ballamont's most captivating feature was the expressive form of her mouth as she spoke, smiled, or just listened.

"Are you a student, Mademoiselle?"

"*Oui*. At the Sorbonne."

"Ah, that explains why you're English is so good. And what are you studying at the University?" I asked.

"I am studying Chemistry," she said.

"Chemistry? That is unusual. Are you going into some scientific field?" I asked.

"In a way. You see I'm from Provence in the Rhone River valley. It is wine country. Our family has been making wine there for generations. I am studying chemistry because I intend to make our wines the best possible. Good enough to compete with the wines of Bordeaux and Burgundy. Good enough to be served in the best Paris restaurants. I want to understand the real mechanisms that affect the wine. Old men like my father just understand from experience. I believe our winery can do better if we employ modern techniques," she said.

"And your father? What does he think?" I asked.

"My father is a sweet man, but he is not yet convinced. However, my mother convinced him that I should go to the university if that was what I wished. He thought I should get married. My mother argued that marriage could wait, intellectual curiosity could not. My mother is a very strong woman and she has a way of manipulating my father," Dominique said with a wry smile.

I smiled also and said, "So you will return to Provence when your studies are completed?"

"Oh yes. I am anxious to apply myself in the business. You see I have learned more than just science in the two years I have been studying. My father is satisfied to just make good wine. I want to make our business more prosperous as well. My father already listens to me more about those areas. He understands I wish to help run our winery and there's less talk of marriage."

"You have brothers and sisters?" I asked.

She hesitated and her eyes moistened slightly. "I had two brothers. Both were killed in the War."

"I am so sorry. I can't imagine how difficult that must be for you and your family. As for myself, I was fortunate enough to survive my experiences in the War. I was a journalist not a soldier so I was not at the same risk."

That led to a discussion about me. She was thrilled to learn that I was a writer and wanted to read the stories I had published. It was at that time that I fully came to grips with my lack of aging. I was explaining my life but had to lie about details that would reveal my true age. I was forty-eight and looked in my twenties, wooing a woman in her early twenties. I told her of my beginnings in the Pennsylvania coalfields, but with a different chronology. No mention of combat in Cuba. My tenure as a New York City reporter was abbreviated. I felt guilty for concealing my real age. I still thought myself only fortunate that I looked so young, not as being a result of some abnormality.

After some food, I convinced Dominique to have a glass of wine. This allowed me to turn the discussion back to winemaking. After two hours, the sun was setting. We both seemed a little surprised at how long we had been talking. Dominique agreed to meet again for lunch the next day.

We had lunch two days straight and dinner several times the following week. I was in love. After so many women, I knew my feelings for Dominique were different. Obviously she was attracted to me, but I had not yet gauged if she felt as strongly as I did.

She was a remarkable woman. Once past our first encounter, we were Dominique and Dillan. She rejected the forced politeness deemed proper between the sexes. She was animated in her conversation and confident in her views. She listened with interest to my views but didn't shy from challenging me.

To my surprise and delight, it was she who suggested our first lovemaking. It was after dinner one night. We were walking back to her flat that she shared with three other women. Stopping, she held me and whispered in my ear, "I love you, Dillan and I want to make love to you. Let's go to your flat. Is it far?"

Dominique was not a virgin, but neither was she practiced in lovemaking. We spent glorious hours learning how to pleasure each other. She never asked how I had acquired knowledge in certain techniques. After a few weeks, she was spending most nights at my flat.

Two months later I asked her to marry me. She said yes, but said that she wished to be married at home in Provence. So in the fall of 1925 we took the train to Avignon. Her parents gave me a warm welcome. I liked them instantly. Almost immediately they accepted me into the family.

Things fell into place. Before leaving Paris I had applied for French citizenship. It was relatively easy since I had good references. I gave my date of birth as 1898. A letter from the Catholic parish in Pennsylvania which gave the birth date and baptism of Dillan Murphy as 1873 was easily altered to '98'. Although I had never attended Mass, owing to my father's antagonism against the Church, the affirmation of my Catholic legitimacy avoided any obstacle with our union by the local priest.

Upon Dominique's matriculation from the Sorbonne in 1927, we left Paris for Provence. Only for Dominique would I have made the move. I was an urban creature. I was part of the literary community of Paris. Now I was going to the rural hinterlands. Thank God it was to winemaking, not something like sheep herding.

It did not take long to fall in love with Provence. Provence was food and wine, and its own special rhythms of life. Once married, we occupied a bedroom in her parent's house. My sense of lost privacy was soon replaced with a new sense of belonging. Aimee, Dominique's mother adopted me as if I were her son. Within days of my arrival, she said to me, "I see how you love my Dominique, how you make her happy. It is easy for me to love you too."

I also quickly adapted to my new role as manual laborer alongside Dominique's father, Pierre Ballamont. We quickly bonded as friends, he discussing wine growing, me talking about New York and Paris, and literature. The manual labor was cathartic.

Pierre had his own take on society and politics. One afternoon after a long day of trimming vines, we sat relaxing with a bottle of wine.

"I wished I would have had all girls, especially if they were like Dominique. Young women are not sent to war. You of course know that I lost two sons in the War. My oldest fell at Verdun, my youngest was gassed in Flanders. I blame not just the Germans but also our own government and the generals. This was not a war that they tried to win. It was a stupid exercise in attrition by generals too incompetent to do other then send tens of thousands of young men to their deaths," Pierre Ballamont said angrily.

After recounting my own experiences in the War, Pierre wept, my descriptions causing him to conjure up thoughts of how his boys must have suffered.

· · · · · · · · · ·

"On that note, I suggest we go to bed. I promise that I will finish my story tomorrow, Allison," Elliot said.

"Very well, Elliot. My head is spinning," Allison said. She kissed his cheek and climbed the stairs to her bedroom.

"Tomorrow I will give you proof that all I have told you is real. Good night, Allison," Elliot said.

The next morning, Elliot was outside drinking his coffee when Allison came down. "You're up early, Elliot."

"My time is short, Allison. "Sleep is secondary."

Allison started to argue about how doctors are consistently wrong, but Elliot declared that he had thoroughly dispelled any chance for error. Too many doctors agreed with the diagnosis.

Elliot prepared omelets for breakfast.

"Elliot, it's so important that I hear about your personal life. What happened to Dominique?"

Elliot exhaled a deep sigh. "Dominique died, otherwise she'd be with me. God I loved her. Loved her for eighteen years. The best years of my very long life."

Elliot continued. "In my memoirs, I tried to tell our love story without devoting an excessive amount of play to those circumstances important mostly only to us. A love story is difficult to tell unless it's against a backdrop of some sort of compelling event. Ominous thunderclouds were gathering in Europe between the world wars, but we were relatively untouched in our rural Provence. Dominique and I had an extraordinary life together, at least until the onset of World War Two.

The winery prospered during the thirties. Dominique slowly took control of the wine making, then eventually the business aspects as well. By some subtle understanding, Dominique replaced her father as the head of the business. I participated, but more as a laborer when necessary. My time was spent chiefly with writing. My novel *Vintage Year* gained modest success. It was essentially a love story. Somewhat autobiographical except for the plot which I fabricated to give the story a skeleton. I became a minor celebrity locally."

"I'm sorry that I don't know your earlier work, Elliot, or should I say Dillan?"

"No reason you should. This was in the thirties. Unless you were Hemingway or Fitzgerald, you weren't in print in the seventies or eighties."

"Where was this winery?" Allison asked.

"Just a few miles from here. That's why I returned to Châteauneuf-du-Pape. Those years I spent here with Dominique were the best of my life. Her parents became mine. The locals adopted me into their community. It was the first place that I could identify as my home. After

New York and Paris, after reporting on crime and wars, the measured rural rhythms here were a tonic to my soul."

Elliot could not help but to smile as he recalled those memories. "You must read my book, *Terroir*. Published in 1932. It's my only other work that doesn't deal with war. Wasn't commercially successful. It's about wine, and food, and love of life. I still reread it to take me back to those times."

He continued, "In the morning I would help in the fields or the winery. Dominique's father taught me how to trim the vines. He was a marvelous guy, at peace with his world, saddened by the loss of his sons, but not bitter. Dominique taught me the technical side of winemaking, gently corrected on occasion by her father's experience. Harvest season in October was long days of backbreaking labor. I loved every minute of it. In the middle of the day we relaxed over lunch prepared by Dominique's mother. It was Aimee Ballamont that taught me basics in Provencal cooking. She made her own cheeses. I learned from her that cheese making was nearly as involved as winemaking. In the afternoon, I wrote. In the evening after dinner, Dominique taught me how to love."

Allison was almost afraid to ask the obvious question as to what happen to Dominique. Elliot answered the unspoken question first.

"I clung to the illusion of my idyllic life here in Provence even as I could see Europe descending into darkness. Hitler and his Nazi Party came to power in Germany in 1933. The Nazi's virulent anti-Semitism screamed on the radio even here in France. In 1936 events escalated. Directly challenging France, German troops occupied the Rhineland. Mussolini invaded Ethiopia in Italy's pathetic quest for colonial territory. In 1936 the Spanish Civil War broke out. Franco's Fascists displaced the republican government. Over the next couple of years that war took on greater significance as a conflict of political ideologies between Fascists and Leftists, and everything in between. The Soviets and the Germans used it as a preliminary bout to the main event. Then with the coming of the Second World War, life changed abruptly for France," Elliot said.

Excerpt from *The Journal of Dillan Murphy* **– Châteauneuf-du-Pape, Provence, France – 1940 – 1944**

Dominique had no illusions about what was happening in Europe. The Sorbonne was the center of Leftist intellectualism in France. There was a significant population of Communists and Socialists among the student body. While she did not identify herself with any particular ideology, she still was decidedly left leaning.

The aggressions of the Fascists in Germany, Italy, and Spain, not to mention the heavily right-leaning factions in France and Britain, provoked Dominique to rants in her frustration. I certainly found the Fascist dictators reprehensible, but that did not mean I saw solutions in the extreme Left. The Communists and Socialists promoted unrealistic social concepts. I made the mistake of arguing the point with Dominique.

"All I'm saying is that Socialism can't define any real workable government, and that Communism is a dictatorship or oligarchy no better than the Fascists," I said.

"How can you make that absurd comparison?" Dominique responded. "The goddamn Fascists are the ones in power, and killing or suppressing anyone in their way. The Fascists could even take over France. We have our share of Fascists here too."

"What about Stalin and the Soviets? How do you categorize that state?" From what I read, Stalin kills more people than anyone else. Is he the alternative to Fascism?" I said, hot into the debate.

Dominique had her fight style up. "Hell no. I knew many Communists at the Sorbonne, and they would say that the Soviet Union does not practice true Communist concepts. Stalin is simply a dictator that has corrupted socialist ideology."

I replied, "Just like the Popular Front in Spain. From the reports, the real reports, not the bullshit the likes of which my friend Hemingway writes, the Leftists are committing the same atrocities as Franco's Fascists," I said. "Same old excuse that anything is acceptable if your cause is righteous."

"You know what you are, Dillan, you're a fucking Anarchist. According to you, all ideologies are bad and no one should govern. You hate governments. You criticize France, the Brits, even the United States," Dominique said.

"No, no. I'm not an Anarchist. Anarchists are the silliest of the lot. They expect everyone to do things collectively with no leadership. I just don't trust government, no matter how it's structured. The concept of power always corrupts," I answered, and then continued. "Government cannot have a collective moral aspect. It's simply there to make things work. If it's good, it's only because of its laws, and the execution of those laws. It's never good because of the collective character of those in the government. The United States system is the fairest because of the foundation of its laws, not because of the people in government. Believe me, politicians there are corrupt also. It's kept in check only because of the law. And then only because a free press keeps a check on the politicians."

We were sitting outside on a warm summer evening. The bottle of wine was finished. Pierre and Aimee had long since retired. Dominique said. "You are a political innocent, *mon cheri*, but I did not marry you for your politics. Perhaps I married you for your skills at lovemaking. No?" We retired to the bedroom to resolve that question.

In 1939, Germany annexed Czechoslovakia, and then a few Months later invaded Poland. In May 1940, Germany invaded France, then Belgium, then the Netherlands and Luxemburg. Within a couple of weeks the Germans had driven the Allied forces off the Continent at Dunkirk and swept over Belgium where they had bogged down in the First World War, twenty-five years earlier. Not this time. In another two weeks, the highly mechanized, fast-moving Panzer Divisions had rolled across northern France and German troops entered Paris.

Everyone in France had known for some time that war was imminent with Germany. Because of Germany's and the Soviet Union's participation in the Spanish Civil War in the late 1930's, some naively assumed that war would be focused on the eastern front between Hitler and Stalin. Equally clear was the fact that Hitler had retooled German's military might in the twenty intervening years from the World War One Armistice. France had not. It therefore fell to Britain to help defend against Hitler's aggression. But no one could believe how swiftly the German Panzer divisions brushed aside French and British resistance and occupied our beloved Paris.

The French government fell. The World War One General, Henri-Philippe Petain became Premier and negotiated an armistice with Germany. Under the agreement, France was divided into occupied and unoccupied zones. The Germans directly controlled the northern and western regions of France, and the entire Atlantic coastline. The semi-autonomous but essentially puppet Vichy Government, with Petain at its head, controlled the central and southern portions of France.

The wooded and mountainous areas in the unoccupied Vichy zone of control became a haven for Communists and Socialists, and for French soldiers that had escaped. They organized into armed resistance cells, calling themselves the Maquis.

Until 1943, our life in Châteauneuf-du-Pape was relatively unchanged. As part of the Vichy state it did not suffer under occupation as did the north since the fall of France in 1940. In 1943 the situation began to change as the Germans started to conscript Frenchmen for labor, and Jews were being sought for deportation.

While in the fields one morning, Pierre and I were approached by a man that emerged from an adjacent hedgerow to the vineyard. The man was carrying a weapon slung over his shoulder.

"Bonjour," the man said and extended his hand. "My name is Jacque Berry. Formerly Captain Berry of the French Army. Now, I once again fight the Germans. I am with the Maquis. I am here to request any help you might give us." Like any insurgency, the Maquis could only survive with the active support of the populace.

"What manner of help?" Pierre asked.

"Food mostly. Any weapons you might be willing to spare."

"We have no weapons, but I think we can manage some food," Pierre said. He did not hesitate in his response. Pierre hated the German occupation and Petain's puppet Vichy government.

Jacque Berry waved his arm and two other men emerged from the shrubbery. Pierre and Aimee loaded up the men with as much provisions as we could spare. Aimee added a couple of blankets. "It's for the cold," she said to the two young men.

As they were leaving, Jacque Berry said. "Merci. If you ever have useful information, leave us a sign." Pointed toward the barn, he said, "Turn that wheelbarrow upside down and place a flower pot on top. Someone will contact you within a day. Viva la France!"

A week later we were having our midday meal when a car and large lorry drove up. There was a loud pounding on the front door. Pierre answered the door.

Outside stood an officer of the Vichy police, the Milice Française, with two armed men in uniform behind him. Through the windows we could see additional armed Milice moving around to the back of the house. The officer pushed his way through the door of the house followed by two of his men.

"Who lives here?" the officer commanded.

Pierre told him. The officer then told his men to bring everyone to the front room.

At this point I must explain about the Milice Française. *Milice* is French for militia. However, they did not act as a militia. It was formed in 1943 when the Germans demanded the French Vichy Government create a more reliable security force to counter increasing partisan activity. At the head of the Milice was a malignant right-wing ex-soldier, Joseph Darnand. After being captured in 1940 by the Germans, he escaped to Nice. Soon after he established a paramilitary group that eventually transformed into the Milice. Darnaud was actually given a German Waffen SS rank, which suggested where his real orders originated.

The Milice became the Vichy equivalent to the German Gestapo. More secret police than military, their mission was to hunt down partisans and roundup Jews for deportation to the East. Like the Gestapo, the Milice would use torture when it suited their needs.

"Papers," the officer barked. All of us handed over our identity documents.

"Monsieur Murphy. What kind of name is that?" the officer asked.

"Irish. I'm of Irish descent. But I'm a French citizen now," I answered.

"Irish. That is good. Ireland doesn't like Britain. However, Monsieur Murphy, I believe we have a problem. You say you are married to this woman?" The officer asked as he held the document up so as to let light come from behind to examine the document carefully. "It says here that you were born in 1898. That would make you forty-five. You look no more than thirty. How is that possible?"

"Perhaps good living?" I answered sarcastically.

The officer glared at me menacingly, intending to intimidate. "I think perhaps because this is not you. Who are you really, Monsieur Murphy? A Jew perhaps? We must get to the truth. Therefore, you will come with us."

Dominique yelled, "No! He is my husband. He is no Jew!"

I tried to calm Dominique saying everything would be all right, while being more scared then I had ever been in the trenches in Flanders. There were stories of torture by the Milice to extract information. There were also stories of deportations to the east. This is what happened to Jews. Supposedly deported to work camps in Germany, but rumors suggested a fate far more sinister.

Dominique brought me a jacket. Unfortunately she also brought my .45 pistol concealed underneath.

I took the jacket from her arm and was horrified to see her pointing the pistol at the officer, no more than five feet away. The Milice officer's mouth dropped open at the sight of the large caliber pistol pointed at him. Stupidly, he reached for his own sidearm. Events then unfolded with everyone in the room reacting.

Dominique shot the officer in the chest twice. One of the Milice soldiers reacted with a burst from his submachine gun. I lunged at him, striking him squarely on the nose with my fist. The force plummeted him into the other Milicien and both went down. I viciously mauled the faces of both men with my fists.

To my horror, I turned around to both Dominique and her mother lying on the floor. Dominique had been hit twice in the abdomen. A large pool of blood was forming on the stone floor. I remember screaming.

Then there was the roar of a shotgun as Pierre shot a Milicien coming through the back door. In a rage, I picked up both my .45 and the submachine gun and bolted out the front door. I crawled under the lorry assuming the remaining Milice soldiers would attempt to leave. Three men came running around a corner of the house straight for the truck. A burst from the submachine gun dropped two of them. The third man retreated, but within seconds, I heard the report of the shotgun again.

Two of the men were not dead. I dispatched them with bullets to the forehead.

When I entered the house, Pierre was on his knees cradling his beloved Aimee and sobbing. I joined him on the floor, stroking Dominique's hair, also weeping in a black despair.

Both of us were on the floor for some time before Pierre finally said. "We will bury them my son."

We buried Dominique and her mother in a corner of the vineyard. Finding the strength was almost unbearable. Pierre struggled to turn the earth with his shovel.

After a silent prayer, Pierre said. "Dillan, we must leave here immediately. The Maquis will help us. I'll gather some provisions; you gather what weapons we can carry. We have only perhaps a few hours to find refuge. We'll leave the signal for Captain Berry, but we can't wait until they show up to contact us."

In the Milicien officer's car I found a hunting rifle with a scope in a leather case. It was a British Lee Enfield .303 with a highly polished stock. Undoubtedly it belonged to the officer. I wondered if it was to hunt game or hunt men.

"I don't know where to find the Maquis, but I would guess perhaps the hills of the Luberon to the east," Pierre said. I was in a daze and followed his instructions without thinking or caring. I am sure I must have seemed in much the same state as those shell-shocked soldiers in the trenches of the First World War.

We took extra petrol from the Milice vehicles and headed east in Pierre's old truck. Eventually abandoning the truck, we hiked into the rugged hills until Pierre could go no further.

After camping out for two nights in the hills, we were eventually approached by the local Maquis and once again met Captain Berry. And so my father-in-law and I joined the ranks of the French Resistance. Pierre was too old to participate on missions. However, I was fit and fuelled by a rage to kill what was now a personal enemy.

■ ■ ■ ■ ■ ■ ■ ■ ■ ■

Elliot stopped his narrative and realized that tears were streaming down his face. "My life was destroyed," Elliot said. "But so were the lives of millions of others. This was wartime under an enemy occupation. Vichy France was little different than the occupied zone that was directly under German control. I could either die or fight. There was no middle ground."

Allison came over and embraced Elliot. His tears flowed quietly. After some moments, Allison said, "I can't imagine seeing my loved one killed before my eyes. My God, Elliot, the events you have experienced. It's overwhelming."

Composing himself, Elliot continued. "I survived because of Pierre. His loss was double that of mine yet he was constantly concerned about my well-being. He was a wonderful old man. Throughout the days in the hills he stoically went about his tasks. At night, he went off to be by himself. I often found him weeping."

Elliot continued. "Unfortunately, life exposed to the elements proved too much for Pierre. He died of pneumonia in the winter of 1943. His companionship had saved me. His death left me truly alone."

"What did you do in the Resistance?"

Elliot looked at her intently. "I killed people. Mostly the Milice. Some Germans."

Allison was slightly shocked by Elliot's matter of fact statement. "How was that? Did it bother you?"

"No, it didn't bother me. Probably it should have. These were not even enemy soldiers. Fascist pigs. They rounded up Jews to be sent east to the Camps. They murdered and tortured people. They deserved killing. I was not troubled about being that instrument." Elliot answered, the bitterness evident in his voice.

"This is where you got the material for *Le Resistance?*" Were you the protagonist Henri in the book? Did you kill that many?"

"Yes. *Le Resistance* grew out of that experience. The story was fiction but most of the events came from personal experience. I found that I had a skill that was uniquely suited to my new circumstances. I practiced with the hunting rifle and found I had a knack for shooting. No one else in our Maquis group could match me. Jacque Berry, the commander therefore put me to good use. I became a long-range assassin. A sniper. Most of my targets were officers. Best trophy was a German Waffen SS colonel. Head shot at over 250 meters."

Excerpt from *The Journal Of Dillan Murphy* – Avignon, France – 1943

After a string of successful shootings at long range, Jacque Berry decided to make selected assassinations their own set of missions. Up to that time, I usually took my sniper shot as just part of a larger mission. If we were going to attack, typically I would take the first shot at a target of opportunity, making my kill and signaling the start of the attack.

Captain Berry created a special assassination team consisting of three others and myself. Two of the others were woman, the other an older man of sixty. One woman was in her late twenties, the other old enough to pass as the wife of the older man. Seeking out high value targets to kill required infiltrating towns and cities. A young man would be suspect since the Germans had implemented obligatory labor service on young French men. The Maquis gained recruits from those refusing to go to Germany and work in factories to support the Nazis war machine. The Milice knew this, so any young man would be a target of suspicion.

I got around the problem by wrapping my left knee in a makeshift brace under my trousers, simulating a bad leg. A war wound if questioned. Our papers were first-rate forgeries.

Perhaps my greatest success was a mission in the city of Avignon in the winter of 1943. The magnificent old walled city on the Rhone River was once the seat of the Papacy in the thirteenth century. It was now the sector headquarters of the Milice with a German Gestapo liaison office. Our mission was to kill the Milice commander. The purpose being to terrorize the Milice command and to show them there was no safe refuge.

The older man and woman team had reconnoitered the vicinity surrounding the Milice police barracks. They found rooms available in an apartment building a short distance down the street from the Milice headquarters.

The younger woman of the team, known as Marie, was a musician, a cellist. She was from Lyon, and she was Jewish. She had been away when the Milice came to their house. Her entire family however was deported east to the camps. Marie was perpetually withdrawn and said little when we were alone. When called upon to play her role however, she was able to retrieve her true personality with an occasional engaging smile.

Posing as man and wife, we rented the room located by the older members of the team. It could not have been better for a sniper position. It was on the second floor and since the street took a slight bend, the view from the room looked directly onto the front entrance of the police headquarters.

Once inside the room, Marie opened the cello case and separated the top of the cello that had been modified to hold the dismantled rifle and scope. Once assembled, I sighted the rifle onto the target, careful not to expose the barrel out the window. 250 meters plus. It would be a fairly long shot, but within my range.

The hard part was the waiting. We might be here for days. Unfortunately Marie was reclusive and poor company. She harbored her own demons. I did not intrude. So we ate our bread and cheese mostly in silence with me sitting in a chair at the window and her on the bed. There was no relaxing. Once I took the shot, we would have to leave immediately.

A German staff car drove up to the Milice Headquarters the next morning. Through the scope I watched an officer exit the car and enter the building. The black uniform was that of a full colonel in the German Waffen SS. For the next hour, I stared intently through the scope waiting for either the Colonel or the Milice Sector Commandant to appear. The Milice Commandant was my assigned mission, but a high-ranking German officer was an attractive target of opportunity.

The question of which target was answered when both came out the front door of the building. As if finding their marks on stage, they stopped to say something to each other.

My first shot caught the Milice commander in the right temple. I ejected the spent round and chambered another with the bolt action. It was a maneuver I practiced at length to maximize the ability to get off successive shots. The stupid German colonel helped by turning from the fallen man to look in the apparent direction of the shot. So he was looking directly in my direction when my second shot hit him below his right eye.

I dismantled the rifle and helped Marie secure it within the cello. Several long minutes passed before we could exit the building. Our other team members had detonated a small bomb under a police lorry behind the barracks as a diversion. Our chances were still probably only fifty-fifty.

Rather than try to immediately escape the city, we exited at the back of the building and circled back around the end of the block to the street in front. The ploy was intended to appear as if we were returning home. Our story was that Marie had been to a fellow musician's house practicing. The story would not hold up under much scrutiny but at least we were not fleeing the scene. In fact, we were approaching the scene.

"Halt!" A Milice soldier yelled. Two others accompanied him with weapons leveled. "Papers!"

We produced our documents and asked what all the commotion was about. The soldier asked what we were doing. Marie answered calmly using our cover story.

"Open the case." The soldier ordered. Marie unfastened the hinges and opened the cover. She pulled the cello and bow out of the case. "Play something," he ordered.

Marie played a few bars of a classical piece. The rifle concealed inside degraded the acoustics of the instrument, but the soldier did not notice anything amiss. As for me, I was not as calm as Marie. I could not stop thinking about the same circumstances when Dominique was killed. In the back of my waistband was the .45 pistol. I had no intention of being arrested in this situation either. The Milice soldiers let us go however.

. . . .

"You were like the Russian sniper in Stalingrad in the book, *Enemy at the Gates*?" Allison asked.

"In some ways I guess," Elliot answered.

"How many would you say you killed?" Allison asked.

"Twenty-three. I can remember each one vividly. Killing people is not something you forget, especially when seen through the lens of a riflescope. Makes it fairly personal."

Allison said *Le Resistance* was perhaps her favorite of Elliot's books. At her prodding, he recounted in some detail those twelve months as a partisan until the Allies reclaimed France in 1944. It was after midnight when he finished that part of his life's story.

"In the end, I came to realize that I suffered from the same perspective that fuels all hatreds justifying the brutalities inflicted upon ones enemies." Elliot added. "In my mind, those that I killed were subhuman, deserving of the worst death. I tried to acknowledge that in the ending of *Le Resistance*."

Allison shook her head. "Amazing. The things you've done. Amazing that you haven't been killed somewhere along this extraordinary long life. You seem to have always gravitated to danger. It's now 1945. The War's over. *Le Resistance* was your first book, at least as Elliot Gaston. It came out around 1980. It was one of my first editing jobs. So what did you do those intervening years? And when did you become Elliot Gaston?"

It's late my dear. Tomorrow I will bring you up to the time you first met me.

Elliot was already up with a cup of coffee when Allison came down to the kitchen the following morning.

"Don't you ever sleep?" Allison asked.

"Seems like no time left. Funny to say that when maybe I have lived longer than anyone," Elliot answered.

"For someone with a supposedly terminal disease, you look remarkably healthy."

"That's what makes this cancer so deceptive. The doctors said there may be periods where I felt fine," Elliot said. "Omelet?"

After breakfast, Elliot suggested a walk. The weather had turned unseasonably warm. "There was a real Elliot Gaston. He was a correspondent for the newspaper *Le Monde*. We met in 1956 in Algiers. I was working for a French news agency, also as a correspondent. We became acquaintances."

"One evening we were having dinner at café popular with Europeans in Algiers. We should have known better with the wave of bombings by the Front de Libération Nationale, the Algerian nationalist political movement seeking independence from France. I was in the toilet when the bomb went off. My colleague was among those killed. I took his passport."

Elliot continued to explain. "You see the real Elliot Gaston bore a very similar resemblance to me, sufficiently such that I later got a new passport without anyone questioning the likeness. I had been concerned for some time about my documentation. In 1956 it made me 58 years old with my fictitious year of birth as 1898. It was getting difficult to justify that age with my appearance. So when poor Elliot was killed, I simply recognized the opportunity."

"So you changed identities as simple as that?" Allison asked.

"Things were simpler in that time. Current technology and concerns about terrorism would make it much more difficult today. Before ever using Elliot's passport, I renewed it, thereby getting my actual photograph and my own fingerprint on the document. Much less scrutiny of the photograph than what you'd get at immigration security entering a country. Surprisingly easy, particularly since the real Elliot Gaston would not be reporting the loss." Elliot answered. "The first time I used it was when I went to Northern Ireland in 1973."

"Hold on Elliot. Northern Ireland? You're losing me. What happened after World War Two?" Allison asked.

"I found it difficult to manage the despair after the War. Like so many others, I lost a loved one, but I had to reconcile that with having to spend endless years grieving that loss. Suicide was considered often during the worst moments," Elliot said.

"I came back to Châteauneuf-du-Pape and bought this place. I tried writing for a few years, but didn't produce anything. Drank too much. Couldn't shake depression. Memories of Dominique dominated my thoughts. Eventually, I found a job as a journalist for the French news agency, Agence France-Presse. It was started by a group of former Resistance fighters, one of which was a colleague in my Maquis unit. I volunteered to cover warzones. Perhaps it was a subconscious death wish."

Elliot went on to explain those years of traveling the globe in search of wars to report on. First there was Indonesia in 1954 where the French were fighting a communist insurgency in their colony. The Elysée Palace spewed out reassuring pronouncements of military superiority that were outright lies. He left Saigon just before the defeat of the French garrison at Dien Bien Phu, proclaiming French impotence in international affairs.

He described going to Kenya to cover the so-called Mau Mau uprising. White landowners were fighting a nationalist insurgency in yet another European colony, this time the British. His novel, *Lion Country*, grew out of that experience.

"In 1956 I returned to France's continuing foreign troubles as she tried to quell rebellion in another of her colonies, Algeria," Elliot said.

"*The Casbah*, of course," Allison remarked, referring to Elliot's novel named for the old part of the city of Algiers.

"Yes, *The Casbah*. I made a few enemies with that book. It all depended on what ideological side you espoused, particularly if you were French. The insurgents were a bunch of ideologues bent on forcing out the French at any cost. Their methods including bombings like the one that killed my colleague, the real Elliot Gaston. The French were committed to holding on to the last visages of empire. Their method was brutality. To my dismay, the French military in Algeria eventually degenerated into acts of torture and summary executions."

"During my time in Algeria, I had become unpopular with my reporting of the French Army's excesses. There were several thinly veiled threats from more than one French officer. I was also getting pressure from the Agency to temper my aggressive pursuit of French atrocities and focus more on the insurgents' acts of terror. It was therefore convenient for them to send me on a short assignment away from Algeria. That assignment was to follow the French Army in their invasion of Egypt along side the British to seize back control of the Suez Canal from the Egyptians."

Elliot continued his narrative. "In the early 1960's, I returned to Saigon to cover the growing American military presence in Vietnam. Wars seem never to end, but just rest for a time until the old antagonisms produce a new generation to take up the conflict. So it was with Vietnam, partitioned by the United Nations in 1954 after the defeat of the French, the Communist North was now fighting South Vietnam."

"In 1967, I was in Israel briefly to cover the Israeli-Arab Six-Day War, or at least the last three days of it. After that, there was a succession of vicious civil wars in Africa."

"The last war I covered for Agence France-Presse, if you can call it a war, was the *Troubles* in Northern Ireland," Elliot said. "I had a fleeting interest to experience my ethnic roots, but it didn't strike any feelings of ancestry in me."

"It was 1973 and the start of the current sectarian conflict. The Irish have been trying to drive the British from the Island for centuries. Crack British paratroops had just killed 14 unarmed Catholic civilians the previous year in Londonderry. As a reporter, you could always rely on the British or the French to be killing people in some other country. Anyway, the incident in Londonderry provided the basis for the Irish Republican Army to gain support among Catholics and begin a bloody insurgency against British control of Northern Ireland."

"What made you quit covering wars as a journalist?" Allison asked.

"From a practical standpoint, it meant changing identities. I now had to assume the identity of Elliot Gaston. Dillan Murphy was now seventy-five by his passport. I wasn't going to be able to pass through security, especially into Northern Ireland. So I went off with a passport in the name of Elliot Gaston, reporting back to the news agency as Dillan Murphy. I couldn't keep that up. So at the least, I had to quit the Agency. "

Elliot continued. "But on an emotional basis, I guess there was a fair amount of burn-out. Certain amount of emotional scarring. You can't continually see that kind of brutality and suffering without losing something in yourself. I hated war, yet was drawn to it for my own reasons. There's nothing more visceral to experience and to write about. For whatever reason, I got it out of my system."

"I have developed some very strong feelings about war," Elliot said. "War is the terrible and ultimate solution to social and economic differences. Its origin is all the base instincts of man – jealousy, intolerance, greed, power over others. It's bred of ethnic and cultural tribalism that seems to exist in all societies. The social grouping becomes the sole body of identification and survival. People have a compelling need to identify with some group for security and validation of one's being."

"Governments and societies always hold up the highest of principles as to why they must destroy the *enemy.* How else to convince young men to risk their lives? And in every war, young men are drawn like moths to the flame for duty, glory, or simply adventure. The ideologues and politicians are only too happy to beat the drum of some corrupted policy to send young men to their death. The seemingly wronged ethnic group always claims righteousness for killing the supposed enemy. Each side prays to their god to help them kill the other. It seems innate in mankind's nature to make war."

Allison said, "That's some rant. But your books are about war, so it holds an important interest for you."

"That's true," Elliot said. "War shapes so much of our history. It's a perfect canvas to paint my stories. Stories about people caught up in these terrible events. I want the reader to experience the characters in these extremes. I developed a real need to write about these events."

"I love your characters, but I also delight in your unkind treatment of some of the major figures of this century. You clearly have a contempt for most governments, and you're not very generous to religion either," Allison said.

"No argument there. If anyone reads history, you come away seeing each side as self-serving, morally corrupt, and often just evil. Contempt isn't a strong enough word. You see the First and Second World Wars were wars of combatants thrown at each other in epic military battles. There were collateral casualties, but still it was mostly one army against another. The conflicts I covered in the fifties and sixties were wars that seemed aimed at whole populations, not just at surrogate armies. They were largely civil wars, even when they crossed political borders. As bad as the horrors of combat are, they shrink in comparison to the bestiality one ethnic group inflicts upon another."

"Enough of my harangue. That also brings us to lunch and the end of my narrative. You know my life from then to now, Allison. On a practical note, when you get back to New York, check on my earlier books authored as Dillan Murphy. Old archives of the *Herald* and the *Times* will also have my byline. Of course that doesn't really prove that I *am* Dillan Murphy, but there is one piece of real proof."

Elliot brought out an ink stamp pad and proceeded to apply his right thumbprint to several sheets of paper. "You will find that my thumb print matches a passport record issued in 1917 prior to my going to France. So what do you think, Allison? Do you believe my story?"

Allison rose from her chair and put her arms around Elliot. "I do, Elliot. As much as my intellect tells me not to, I do believe you. I've watched you tell me pieces of your life for several days. It could never be a fiction."

"No, but I could be a lunatic," Elliot offered.

"I don't think so. I've known you for over twenty years. You're not delusional," she answered.

"So that you have no linger doubts, check out my books as Dillan Murphy. You know my writing. Read them and see if they're me. You must also check out the fingerprint. That's the only absolute evidence I can offer."

"I will, Elliot. But more importantly, I'd like you come back to New York with me. We'll get you to the best specialists on treating the leukemia. You can stay with John and I. Please, Elliot?" Allison said.

Elliot embraced her. "Allison, I've been to the best specialists in Paris. New York won't change the diagnosis. I know your offer to stay with you is genuine and I love you for it. But I won't have myself as an invalid. I mean to stay right here as long as I can manage. Provence has been my home for a good deal of my life."

"I understand. I'd probably feel the same way. Tell you what; I have to be in London in a couple of months. I'd like to come back down here to see how you're getting along," she said.

"I'd love that," Elliot said and kissed her cheek. "Let's open a very good bottle of Bordeaux and decide on where to go to dinner since this is your last night."

"That sounds wonderful, Elliot. But you haven't told me everything about your current life. Ever since I've known you there seems to have been no woman in your life. Let's see, I met you probably in 1985. You were – you would have been 112 years old? My God that sounds absurd to say. But anyway, you were ancient then. If you'll permit me an indelicate question – are you, or were you, whatever......still sexually active?" Allison asked, a hint of blushing apparent.

Elliot laughed with genuine amusement. "The answer to your question is yes. The fact is I am the age you see, not the chronological age. I have had a few affairs over these last several decades. I have been in love more than once."

Allison could not help a broad grin. "I'm sorry, Elliot, but the vision just struck me of someone over a hundred screwing." With that they both laughed.

"I'm sure I have disappointed several women, and I know my own heart was broken over those same times as well. I knew what it was like to be so in love and connected as I had been with Dominique. But I realized the insurmountable problems of my abnormal longevity in a permanent relationship. I was simply afraid to go there. I confess to having lost so much," Elliot said.

"No one at the moment?" Allison asked.

Elliot thought for a moment before answering, "There's a woman in Orange I see on occasion. A widow. A real estate agent. Loves classical music."

"Ah ha. I knew it. Young and voluptuous I suppose? Allison asked.

"You are obsessed with sex," Elliot responded jokingly. "Yes, my lady friend is very attractive, however she is over fifty."

Elliot and Allison had a wonderful evening. They laughed and enjoyed each other's company. Elliot's story and his illness were not discussed.

Elliot drove Allison to the Marseille Airport the next morning. A drizzling rain and gray sky added to the gloom. It was a tearful goodbye for both.

That was the last time Allison Kryszka's saw Elliot Gaston.

Within a month after her return from Provence, Allison was convinced that Elliot Gaston was inexplicably Dillan Murphy, born in 1873. She had tracked down copies of Murphy's novels. She knew Elliot's writing style intimately and she could see his voice in Murphy's books. Church records in Schuylkill County, Pennsylvania confirmed a Dillan Murphy's birth and the death of his mother. It took a private investigator to secure the old finger print record of the young newspaper correspondent of World War One from old government archives. A lab confirmed the match to the prints she had witnessed

Elliot making for her. A second expert opinion left no doubt.

Allison was trying to determine how she should proceed with handling Elliot's massive journal. Who could she get to edit the manuscript? How to go about publishing it? Call it non-fiction, or just not declare it as such? She had been wrestling with the problem ever since she had left Provence.

One afternoon she received a bulky envelop at her New York office. It was addressed from Aix-en-Provence, France. There were a number of legal looking documents. The cover letter read:

Dear Mademoiselle Kryszka:

It is with regret that I must inform you of the apparent death of Monsieur Elliot Gaston. Monsieur Gaston regrettably appears to have died in a boating accident near Marseille approximately two weeks ago. The circumstances are not entirely clear, but it appears that Monsieur Gaston may have fallen overboard. A small powerboat, rented by Monsieur Gaston, was found miles out in the Mediterranean. Although, no body has been found, the police feel that Monsieur Gaston may have fallen overboard with the engine running. The boat was found without any fuel remaining and the throttle in the power position. There was no indication of foul play, but some evidence that liquor may have played a part.

Monsieur Gaston has not been officially declared dead, however Monsieur Gaston left specific instructions with our law firm. Those instructions state that in the event of his death, or reason to assume his death, we were to execute certain transactions on his behalf in which he invested me with power of attorney. Essentially, I am executing Monsieur Gaston's last will and testament. Enclosed you will find an itemized list of assets that Monsieur Gaston wished you to have, and all necessary legal documents. Monsieur Gaston has also included a sealed envelope addressed to you personally.

Please do not hesitate to contact me if I may be of any assistance. My sincerest condolences for your loss.
Respectfully,
Henri Randal
Attorney at Law

Allison cried out after reading just the opening line. When her secretary rushed in to see what was wrong, Allison was crying and said, "I'm ok, just some bad news. Hold my calls and shut the door please." It was several minutes before she opened the sealed envelop from Elliot.

Dearest Allison,
When you read this, Allison, I will be gone. However, I had to leave you with this before I left this very long life behind. There are two important things that you need to know. Forgive me if this hurts you, which I fear it will. Nonetheless, I feel compelled to offer a confession. But first I must tell you a brief story. A story about your mother.
I met Marie Kryszka in 1956, in Paris. I was having dinner alone at a restaurant in the Latin Quarter. At an adjacent table, your Mother was dining alone. She obviously did not speak French, and her English was heavily accented. There was some difficulty communicating with the waiter, so I offered my assistance. Admittedly, I was attracted to your Mother. She was an elegant beauty. Engaging her in English, I quickly recognized her intellect. Small talk revealed she was a writer so we obviously connected. The short version is that we connected on a much deeper level. We spent three days together in Paris. And yes, we made love endlessly during those three days.
Unfortunately, Marie left Paris. She was married and felt remorse from our brief affair. I learned this from a note she left. See begged me not to try to find her. I couldn't at any rate since I knew only that she was going to the United States. To this day, I can't watch <u>Casablanca</u> and watch Bogart and Bergman replay the same story as your mother and me.

It was thirty years later that I again heard from your mother. Again by a letter. It was posted from an attorney with instructions to locate me after her death. It was in that letter that she confessed that you were my daughter. She trusted me to decide if I would tell you or not. I decided that would not be fair to you. I was a complete stranger. You had your own life. And I had my 'special problem' that would eventually complicate any relationship. So I did the next best thing by creating a connection with you as my agent. Glad you took me on. I have watched your career with pride.

Don't grieve for me. I've lived two lifetimes. It has been my fortune to be able to define my life and live it on my terms. Most people cannot. I went out my own way, not wasting in pain from a terrible disease. Imagine the things I've seen and experienced. I don't think I wasted my opportunities. From a poor coal miner's son, to a modestly successful writer, to experiencing the great events of the twentieth century, that's more than a full life. I say with some immodesty that I've acquired a measure of wisdom. Wisdom is not understanding some universal truth; it's the thoughtful reflection of one's life experiences and the ability to integrate those experiences into some larger understanding. I've accomplished a lot, now I'm tired.

Remember your mother fondly. She was an extraordinary woman. I knew she was Polish, but I learned only in her letter that she was also Jewish, and survived Auschwitz-Birkenau concentration camp. She did not relate any details of that experience, but the world knows the horrors inflicted on those that passed through those gates. She said your father, the real father that raised you all those years, had died a couple of years earlier. I assume he was a special man for her to have been that devoted, but she did not talk about him either. She gave only the brief explanation that he was also in the concentration camp and she was indebted to him for saving her life.

On a practical note, you will find a copy of my Will enclosed, properly witnessed and notarized. Go to my attorney in Aix-en-Provence as indicated. You are my sole heir. There's not a lot; a modest bank account, all rights to my copyrights, the property here in Provence. Consider keeping it. I believe you enjoyed your time here. It's a marvelous refuge with rhythms from an earlier time.

I hope you find someone special in your life, Allison. You talk about John but somehow I sense that your relationship with him is more intellectual than emotional. Forgive me for being presumptuous and fatherly. But on that note, I must also point out what may not yet be obvious to you. With the revelation of my paternity, you must consider that you may also have my affliction. Not the cancer, but the abnormal longevity. You are almost fifty years old, when you look in the mirror, Allison, don't you wonder why you look only thirty?"

I regret that we could not have been father and daughter. I may have made a mistake by not telling you years ago, but I'm not going to dwell on that. I loved you remotely. I cherished those times we were together.

Live your life fully, Dear. If that is to be an unusually long life, I hope that I may have given you some survival insights. Think fondly of me.

Love,
Your Father

Allison stared out her office window into the gray sky over the towering buildings of Manhattan. She did not move for some time.

■■■■■■■■■■

A man in his late fifties with salt and pepper graying hair exited the train in the city of Ronda, in the south of Spain. He hailed a taxi, giving the driver an address near the center of town not far from the historic bullring and the famous bridge over the gorge.

"Do you come to visit Ronda?" the driver asked in heavily accented English.

"Perhaps to live here. I was here a very long time ago," the man answered, his English carrying a marked French accent.

"Ah, Ronda does that to those who visit here. And what is your business if I might ask, Señor?"

"I write books mostly."

"You sound French, Señor?"

"Yes, I guess you'd consider me French."

"*No habla Espanol*?" the driver asked.

"No, only English and French," the man answered. "I will have to learn Spanish."

"Ah, it is *dificil* to learn a new language. Once you are older it takes a long time. I learned English to drive taxi. Took many years."

"Well, I have a lot of time," the man answered.

THE END

By Douglas Clark

"Men prefer fragrans feminae to any other aphrodisiac, even when they don't know it."
      Robert A. Heinlein, science fiction author

Oh shit, was the first thought as I awoke. Sun was seeping through the blinds. There was already heavy traffic on the street below my second floor flat in the Latin Quarter of Paris. My head hurt from all the wine I consumed the previous night. Dominique, my live-in girlfriend was snoring in a deep sleep. Her bare breasts were enticing but I was clearly not up to anything more than just trying to return to the land of the living. I needed water, coffee, and to take a piss, not necessarily in that order.

I stumbled into our small kitchen. I had been in France less than two years but was already addicted to espresso. Two shots got me going; a third was enjoyed with a light breakfast pastry or toast. It was especially effective medicine for hangovers.

It was Sunday. The sun disappeared around noon, as Dominique and I were about to walk about and get lunch. A light rain started. We opted to go to a movie. It was a typical artsy French film with moody characters and no plot. However, it had particularly erotic lovemaking scenes.

Halfway into the movie Dominique started rubbing my leg. She soon moved to rubbing my growing erection. The next thing I felt was her unzipping my fly. I looked quickly about to see if anyone was watching, but there were few people in the theater for this early matinee. She was breathing audibly as the woman on the screen was experiencing cunnilingus.

"Touch me," she whispered.

I slipped my hand under her skirt and panties. She was already wet.

We touch and probed each other while watching the woman go through protracted attentions from the man's lips and tongue. I had only a vague sense of what was happening on the screen.

"Let's go home. I want that," Dominique said.

My fingers were wet with her juices. I put them to my nose. Her scent intoxicated me.

I did my best to stuff my erection back into my pants and zip up.

Back at the flat, we duplicated the oral lovemaking of the movie. It was a great rainy afternoon.

"I have an idea, Dominique." I poured her the last of the bottle of wine and went about opening another.

"And what's that, Mon Cheri?"

"Your smell. You know how it arouses me."

"My smell? What do you mean my smell? My skin? My perfume?"

"No, I mean your pussy. Especially when you're aroused."

"Are you sure you don't mean my taste, Mark?"

I grinned, "Yeah that too. But I mean your smell. Both I guess. Taste and smell kind of work the same. At least they work together."

"Never mind the technical shit. So what's the idea?"

But I probably should explain what it is that I do before going on with my story. My name is Mark Nichols. I'm a staff chemist for a French cosmetics firm, working in product development. At twenty-eight, what I lack in experience I make up for with academic credentials – a PhD in chemistry from M.I.T. with my thesis in the mechanics of the creation of free molecules from emitting substances and the mechanisms of receptivity and recognition by living organisms. Simply put, I am an expert in how smell works. With that expertise, I was clearly not destined to work in petroleum or industrial chemicals.

Henri's de Montmartre recruited me out of graduate school. Henri's is a high-end market French cosmetics and fashion firm. Why an American? How many graduate chemistry students specialize in smell – academically that is?

I thought maybe that I had put myself into a restrictive field. There was no career plan, only an intellectual interest in how smell works. I always had a highly developed sense of smell so I was inherently interested. At any rate, the pay is ok. Better yet, I get to live on the Left Bank in Paris and have a knockout looking girlfriend. Not bad for a kid from a working class family from Cincinnati.

Enough. Back to my story.

"I've been thinking about this for some time," I said. "What if I could duplicate your smell in a cologne or perfume?"

Dominique laughed hard enough to draw her to tears.

"A perfume that smells like pussy? That's the worst idea I've ever heard. I've put my finger inside my pussy and smelled it. No woman's going to want to smell like that, you idiot."

I was not to be deterred. "Two things. First of all, it's to interest men. It's probably a primal response to the female. Second, it won't smell exactly like pussy. I think I can identify the key chemistry and convey it over an innocent overt smell. A couple of companies in the past tried introducing a male scent that was supposed to entice woman by its primal response. They didn't get it right. One brand was called Musk. Smelled like old socks. Men didn't like it. Neither did women."

"I have no idea what you're talking about. All I know is that no woman is going to make herself smell like her pussy."

Whatever came of it, it would be interesting research. The first part started a few days after I had introduced the idea to Dominique. In a high state of arousal, I interrupted our lovemaking to swab a generous amount of her vaginal secretions. Dominique was extremely pissed. She threatened to throw me out of bed but the state of her passion and persuasions with my mouth were sufficient inducements to move past the interruption. She called me a fucking weirdo after she came. Many a scientist has taken greater risks to advance knowledge.

My great idea did not prove easy to develop. It took the better part of a year and long after-work hours in the lab. Harder yet to cover these extra hours with explanations related to official projects. My boss, Dr. Claude Vallot would explode if he knew I was working on a nonauthorized project. Dr. Vallot and I were not real close. Probably because he was a prick.

Beyond the hard work, it was also necessary to win over Dominique to assist in the research. Swabbing was becoming a common part of our lovemaking. She was also interested in understanding the principles of the research. Dominique was the ultimate research assistant. Lovemaking had never been so frequent.

"I think I have it, Dominique," I said to her one evening. I had not let on that I was that close. "Smell this." I handed her a small bottle.

She looked at me and grinned. Opening the stopper, she dabbed a small amount of the clear liquid on her finger and carefully brought it to her nose. "Not bad. Smells like some sort of flower. What is it?"

"What you smell is actually a combination of the essence of several flowers. No pussy smell?"

She tried another sample and took a larger whiff. "No. Flowers. Subtle. Not bad. So what's the deal?"

"Thing is, there's an underlying odor that you can't really smell, if that makes any sense. It's almost subconscious, but it's there. I can tell."

"What do you mean?"

"Well, it's a synthesized chemical version of your pheromones that rides underneath the overt odor. I can't detect it by actual smell either. But it arouses me. I can inhale a couple of breaths and start to get hard. I can feel the arousal immediately without anything else acting as a stimulus."

"What are pheromones?" Dominique asked.

I explained that pheromones are secretions that are intended to affect the behavior of another organism. They're common with lots of animals and insects. I tried to explain in layman's terms how receptor cells in the nasal passage react in complex combinations to form a unique signature for that odor.

"I don't understand any of that," Dominique said. She tried another smell. "You're sure this is what's arousing you?"

"I think so. I've tried it over the last week. Affects me every time. Problem is I need more confirmation. I need more subjects to run a small-scale clinical trial."

"Men you mean?"

"Right. Can you get some of your girlfriends to try this?"

"I assume you mean the ones that want to get laid? I'll do it tomorrow. Do I have them try it on their boyfriends, or just see what it does to strangers?"

"Both. You manage the tests."

"Very well. Then let me begin," Dominique applied strokes of the mixture along each side of her neck and kissed me hard on the mouth.

We made love but it was not a valid experiment of my new invention considering Dominique's aggressive attentions with her mouth.

The next couple of weeks were exciting as Dominique conducted her experiments. She was a marketing professional with a wide circle of friends. I was impressed with her methodology and organization of what would be the first market trials of my product.

It took only a few days before results started to come in.

From Evelyn, ten years older than Dominique, married ten years, quote: 'Maurice has made love to me every other night since I tried your perfume. Where can I buy a liter?'

From Patricia, computer programmer, married to a computer programmer, both qualified geeks, quote: 'My god, Dominique, I had oral sex for the first time.' It's better than wine. What is this perfume?'

From Francis, pretty, party girl, frequents bars, quote: 'It's like attracting bees to a flower. I get my pick. And they do anything I like.'

There were a few others that were not so sure of the results, but would continue to report back to Dominique. Were the superlative results a placebo effect? We waited. Over the next several weeks continued feedback confirmed I had something.

Marie: 'Dominique, it has to be this perfume you gave me to try. Charles has never been this affectionate. That's all I will say on the subject. But I need more of this perfume!'

Daniel: 'I like your perfume, Dominique. It works very well if you know what I mean. When can I get more?'

Kathleen; 'Hard to tell if it was the perfume, but Jacque made love to me for the first time at my cousin's house in the country.'

"This stuff is out of sight, Mark. So now what?" Dominique said.

"I'm going to have Eric look at it, unofficially."

Eric Martineau was French and a good friend. He also worked at Henri's de Montmartre, in the marketing department. We had gone out a couple of times with Eric and his girlfriend Marta. At lunch the next day I gave Eric my remaining quantity. I told him the real attraction of the perfume.

"You're fucking kidding. You mean this stuff smells like pussy? Let's see." He pulled the stopper out, dabbed a small amount on his finger, and applied it on his upper lip. He then inhaled deeply.

"Odd smell. Not unpleasant. Certainly doesn't smell like pussy."

"Of course not. The female smell is there in the form of very specific chemical molecules. There are other tones that mask the direct association with the scent of the vagina. Nonetheless, it can still act on the male brain. "

"Ask Marta to try it. See if it affects you. Have a couple of her friends try it too."

"Very well, Mark. I shall attempt to be most scientific. I will see if it makes me as you say, hornier."

That was Friday. Monday morning Eric called me to invite me to lunch.

"Let me tell you about my weekend, my friend. I did not believe that your perfume had any special powers. Neither did Marta, but she said it smelled good and she'd try it out. We had planned a drive into the country. A picnic. Lots of wine. Just relax. Your perfume started to work on me, Mark."

Eric continued recounting the weekend. "I tell you, I was getting hard as we drove. Marta wasn't even doing anything. She had a simple sundress on. I looked over at her cleavage, looked at her legs, and then got so hard it distracted my driving. After a time, Marta could tell. Without the details, let's say by the time we found an area for a picnic, we were ready.

"We left the food and took our blanket behind a hedgerow. Holy shit, Mark, we must've fucked for an hour out there in the sun. Great afternoon, my friend, but Sunday was more of the same. Saturday might've been other things, but Sunday left me convinced. Marta says women would kill for this. And she's not giving any to her girlfriends."

"So you agree this has got potential."

"Potential? Enormous I should think. Henri's could stand to make a fortune. Problem is what to do next my friend."

"We could bypass my boss and go straight to your boss, Eric?"

"Ah, my American friend. That may happen in the States but not at a French firm. Not if you value your career. Oh, they would develop the product but it would be the end of you and me. You've got to at least try to run it through your department head."

I knew my friend was right but I did not hold out much coming from trying to promote my invention with Claude Vallot. After drafting my report and formulation details, I approached him two weeks later. It turned out worse than imagined.

I had requested an appointment just like a good European staffer. I gave him my report. I expanded upon my adhoc testing. I had also developed another small batch and gave Vallot a small vial.

Vallot accepted the vial but made no attempt to open it or the report.

"I would like to say I am surprised Mister Nichols, however, you have been consistently resistive to following procedures during your employment here. This is not an authorized project. You use company resources on your own pet project then expect acceptance, perhaps even praise for this concoction of yours. Instead, I'll let this go by with only a reprimand."

"A what? A reprimand! You haven't even looked at my invention. I tell you what you are; you're a fucking bureaucrat. We don't create anything really new here because you won't try anything. You wouldn't be able to identify a marketable fragrance if somebody shoved it up your nose."

"That's enough Mister Nichols. Out of my office!"

I attempted to retrieve the vial and copy of the report on his desk, but Vallot quickly picked them up. "Company property Mister Nichols. I'll keep these."

"You fucking little prick. Give them back to me now!"

"You're terminated, Nichols. Fired, I believe they say in America. Now leave," Vallot said and picked up the phone requesting security.

I should have hit him but things were bad enough without going to jail for assault. Security ushered me out.

When I got back to the flat, I called Eric and told him he was an idiot and so was I for taking his stupid advice. When Dominique got home I told her and somehow we got into an argument. I had just screwed up my life and was not sure who to be angry with.

Dominique was distant over the next couple weeks. Eric did not call. And I had to find a new job soon, both for money and to stay in Paris. What I found only made me more depressed. Assistant chemist at a soap manufacturer. Not top of the line either. My job was quality control making cheap fucking bar soap and laundry products. A new career opportunity to learn a different technology.

Four months later I heard from Eric for the first time. He was trying to patch up things. Asked the usual about how things were. Told him they sucked, but I wasn't mad at him. We arranged to meet for drinks the next day.

After a couple of drinks and more small talk, Eric got around to his other reason for contacting me. "Something else I just found out, Mark. Looks like they're moving forward on your perfume."

"What do'ya mean, moving forward?"

"Trails. My boss called a marketing strategy meeting to introduce this *new product* the lab had developed. Initial trials were promising. He was vague about why the new product was unique. Except I could read between his innuendoes about sexual allure and reaching primal stimuli. It's your stuff, Mark! The fuckers are taking your idea and developing a product. Sounds like they're going to put one helluva lot of money into marketing if the tests continue to return results."

"That's great news, Eric. And I get no credit of course."

"In the marketing packet it said we have applied for a patent. It also listed as the inventor your old boss, Claude Vallot."

"Figures. The guy's not only an asshole but also a thief."

"I did some checking with Legal. Doesn't matter whose name is shown as the inventor. If it was designed using Company's resources, the inventor is a name only. All rights get assigned to the Company."

"It's not the money. No. Yes it is. If it wasn't for that prick Vallot, I would have an advanced position and probably a higher salary, not to mention the credit for a major product invention if it's successful. So it matter's one helluva lot whose name is on that patent."

"Listen, I'm sorry to be the one to give you this news. I really wanted to see you and get back together as friends."

I slapped him on the back. "I've missed you too my friend. It's been a tough few months. You know, Dominique and I split up."

"Ah, Mark. I'm so sorry. What happened?"

"I still talk to her. It's my fault. I've been so pissed at everything; I didn't see how it was affecting us. She said she couldn't take my constant anger. I wasn't good to be around. Dragging her down. Bottom line, I couldn't argue what she was saying."

Tears rolled down my cheeks and Eric put his arm around me.

I saw Eric a few more times over the next couple of months. He kept me abreast of developments with *my* product. It had a name, Parfum de Femme. Henri's de Montmartre was preparing a high intensity market introduction to start in Europe. The plan was to establish a high profile European acceptance, then move to the U.S. market. From there, they would expand into Asia. The strategy being based on the Americans' love of things European and the Asian love of things American.

Over the next six months, I made soap and Henri's made a fortune on my invention. Parfum de Femme was a major success. Eric's boss had designed the right campaign to promote the best artificial aphrodisiac on the market. Disguised as perfume, Parfum de Femme was able to get the highest prices in the industry. Its sexual attributes were suggested only subtly in the advertising, and never expanded in any form of copy. Henri's placed ads only in the top fashion magazines, and sold only to high-end retailers.

More populace magazines began to publish pieces. The reputation for Parfum de Femme to attract men's attentions was making its way into popular print.

Here I was making soap and Henri's de Montmartre was making millions on my invention. Worse yet, that fuck Vallot was getting the credit. I cannot say that I planned my next step which was retaliation against the cosmetics firm Henri's de Montmartre, and that shit, Claude Vallot. The idea just occurred to me over drinks with Eric.

"So it seems that Parfum de Femme is really taking off," I said to Eric.

"No shit, Mark. It's everything you claimed. It's fucking fantastic. Orders can't be filled fast enough. Revenues increase every day."

I laughed with real gusto to the point of choking on my wine.

"What? What the hell is so funny?"

Calming down, I looked earnestly at Eric. "Eric, this is fucking great."

"Great? You've been fucked over and you say it's great?"

"What's so funny is that the origin of Parfum de Femme is not what you think."

"What do'ya mean, Mark? Parfum de Femme works. I know first hand."

"Yeah, Eric, I know what Parfum de Femme is, what it does. Remember, I invented it. But I have a confession. I didn't invent it the way I told you."

"What are you talking about? "

"Listen, Eric, the origin wasn't Dominique. It wasn't even a woman."

Eric looked hard at me. "Not a woman? What then?"

"Well it certainly started out from a woman. Dominique, to be specific. I had been interested in the mechanics of how smell triggered sexual arousal. Once I discovered the baseline chemistry from Dominique's samples, I was able to achieve the chemical equivalent without the human female material. I simply experimented with various animal materials to provide quantity. Obviously you could never extract enough real material from women to make commercial quantities. But my synthesized alternative works exactly the same way on the male brain as a woman's real pheromones, and achieves the same effect."

"What animal materials?" Eric asked.

"Well---what ultimately worked was bovine."

"Bovine? You mean pigs."

"Yes. A particular species however,"

"Yeah, but still a pig. So how did you create this shit from a pig?"

"Vaginal secretions. Just like from Dominique. I synthesized the secretions to produce the functional chemistry."

Eric laughed until his side hurt and tears rolled down his cheeks. The other bar patrons looked at us. Once he gathered himself, Eric said, "You made this stuff from a sow in heat?"

Having said that, Eric fell into another fit of laughter.

"Pigs and humans have a lot in common physiologically," I said somewhat lamely.

"Jesus, Mark, this is great. The hottest perfume on the market and you tell me it comes from a fucking pig's pussy? Parfum de Femme is really Parfum de Porc?"`

My guess was that the patent application made no mention of the origins of the enzymes I used. It couldn't. Once the patent was issued and available to the public, they couldn't reveal that its source was of such lowly origins. They would have to have described it chemically. At least a close approximation."

"Of course they wouldn't admit to that. The patent will have been fudged,"

"What is the meaning of *fudged*, Mark?"

"Slightly altered. Slightly obscured. Hide the truth. Tell me, Eric, what would happen if the marketplace learned that Parfum de Femme was perfume made from a hog, no matter what it made men do?"

"I don't know, but it would be like setting a bomb off at Henri's."

Eric and I polished off a couple of more drinks before calling it a night. We were both drunk. I wasn't too drunk to think about bombs though.

I woke up early the next morning. No hangover. A glorious sunny morning. I strolled down the Boulevard Saint Germain and found a café to have *petite dejeuner* and enjoy the Latin Quarter. This was what Paris was all about. But this morning was also glorious because I now had a purpose and direction.

I missed Dominique and I missed my high-class job. Getting even with Henri's would not get either one back. However, revenge is more about self-esteem than justice. A court might satisfy Justice but self-esteem can only be satisfied by personal action. Whatever the philosophical bullshit, I felt alive for the first time in weeks. The soap

maker shall rise up to smote the mighty fashion house of
Henri's de Montmartre,

Over several croissants and coffees I spent a marvelous morning of plotting. Three days later I took step one
to drive a stake through the heart of my former employer. After some work, I found the contact I had been
searching for through the Internet. After a flurry of e-
mails, I enticed him sufficiently to agree to meet me in
Paris.

Peter Barnes. Reporter. Yellow journalist extraordi-
naire with the British tabloid the Daily Mirror. We met at
a good Left Bank restaurant since he was paying.

After a sip of wine, Barnes got down to business. "Let
me understand what you're trying to sell here, Mister
Nichols. You claim that you actually developed this new
perfume sensation Parfum de Femme while working for
Henri's de Montmartre as a chemist, and that you were
fired? And you have something that would shatter the
image of this product? And you want money in return
for the story?"

"That's correct."

"Well, Mister Nichols, we checked you out. You've
got the credentials all right. Impressive even. And we
confirmed you did work for Henri's de Montmartre here
in Paris. What I want to know is why you want to destroy your former employer?"

"That's simple. I invented this seemingly great product. Did it on my own. My idea, my work. Then this boss
of mine not only fires me but steals my work, claims it as
his own invention. This guy's an idiot with no vision, a
bureaucrat with some academic credentials. I would
doubt that I am the first that he has done this to."

"But you're attacking Henri's?"

"They put Vallot where he is. They can accept re-
sponsibility for him. It's just business. Same on my part."

"So is this for revenge or money, Mister Nichols?"

"First, I got fired. Second, I'm looking to be paid for this. Third, why the fuck do you care why I'm doing this?"

"Just to test the voracity of the story if you will, Mister Nichols. When you understand the motivation, you can better judge the truth of what someone is telling you. So how do you convince me of the worth of your story?"

I was prepared for the question. "By more than one account, Parfum de Femme has grossed the equivalent of over £15,000,000 in less than six months on the market just in Europe. Sales continue to grow in Europe. The American market introduction just two months old has equaled that. Can you imagine sales when they eventually hit the full U.S. potential? And then there's Asia. Can you imagine how the Asians will take to this? No reason it won't be around for a very long time.

"So imagine the impact if certain information were to destroy its market image. It would be a very big story. Better yet for you in the tabloids, the story would go on for some time."

"If your information is what you claim, the Daily Mirror would be prepared to pay you."

"How much?"

"Whoa, Mate. Depends on what you've got. And can you back it up?"

"How 'bout this Mister Barnes. You sign an agreement to pay me £15,000, if you publish the story using my information. If after thirty days you have not paid me, then I am free to peddle it to someone else. Once it's published elsewhere you can publish what you like. You can't lose. You get an exclusive for a reasonable price if my story proves worth it. If not, you can always jump on somebody else's bandwagon. The fifteen thousand gives you exclusive rights for thirty days after you publish."

"Interesting offer, Mister Nichols." Barnes was silent for a few moments. "It's a deal then. I will have an agreement prepared and faxed to me in a couple of hours. Shall we get together again say around five at my hotel?"

"Fine. I'll be there," I said and left. I went back to my flat to work on putting together the material for Barnes. As anxious as I was about what I was about to do, I was energized as well.

Over a bottle of wine, I laid out all the details to Barnes. I gave him copies of all my notes detailing the technical composition of Parfum de Femme and its origins, processing steps to synthesize the critical components, and tests.

"Christ, this is one helluva story, Mister Nichols. But no one at the paper will be able to understand even a fraction of this technical stuff. I certainly can't. What in here proves that the origin is a pig's vagina?"

"Simple. You see this string of diagrams on page twenty-four?" I said flipping through my notes. "The molecular structure of this enzyme is unique to a particular species of hog known as a Berkshire. I tried several species but Berkshire was clearly a better source. I am sure that Henri's did not identify the origin of the molecule, or the method of synthesizing it in their patent application. If I were them, I could think of a number of ways to phony it up."

"So how could we defend its origin as being from your Berkshire hogs?"

"Easy. Run a DNA test on a bottle of the perfume. The DNA material is still there in those molecules. There are actually three separate molecular structures, all from the hog. Everything else is inorganic. Buy some Parfum de Femme and run the test before you publish."

"We'll do that, Mister Nichols, straightaway. But tell me this, do you think you can thrust this stick into the eye of Henri's de Montmartre without them fighting back?'

"You worried about lawsuits, Mister Barnes?"

"No. The Daily Mirror is just publishing a story based upon factual information. Information that Henri's can't refute in court. But how will you defend them going after you? Isn't this violating some confidentiality agreement you must have signed? Industrial sabotage? Would seem to be all manner of reasons to sue for damages."

"Damages? What assets do I have? But that's irrelevant anyway. They won't sue. How could they? Can you imagine the media attention focused on the proceedings? I would testify with the same evidence I just gave you. What would they counter with? Like you, I can prove my case with DNA testing. If Henri's pursues legal action against me, it only makes things worse for them. Kind of hope they do. That's revenge, not business, Mister Barnes."

"I can see there's more to you than these scientific scribblings, Mister Nichols. We'll do the DNA tests. If they're as you suggest, we'll thrust that stick into the eye of the house of Henri's de Montmartre."

I rose and shook hands with Barnes and left his hotel room. There was a great relief. The relief of knowing where you were going and having initiated that first step was liberating. Life wasn't yet good but it was headed somewhere.

I don't care what anyone says; when you've been shit on, revenge is sweet. It was on the front page of the London Daily Mirror two weeks from my interview with Barnes. Barnes had called a few days before and told me they were going with the story. The DNA tests confirmed my assertions. Better yet, £15,000 was deposited into my bank account the day before the article was published.

The lead headline read, '*SEX PERFUME ACTUALLY FROM PIGS*'. Unlike most tabloid stories, they went on to give a pretty accurate assessment of the origin of the invention.

Within days, other European tabloids had picked up on the story. The Daily Mirror was still running articles, which having exhausted the facts in the first publication, were now becoming bizarre in their contrived fabrications. The real test would be if the legitimate press investigated and published. That might be unlikely since I was not named in the article. Besides the Daily Mirror, only those at Henri's would connect me as the source.

I had my answer sooner than expected. It was a Friday. Long day at the soap factory. I was looking forward to a nice wine and special dinner. I pushed back the thought that I was by myself. I missed Dominique, but if you had to be alone, there was nothing to compare with relaxing in the Latin Quarter. I loved Paris. I might even get lucky.

I did not get lucky however. Waiting outside my apartment were two suits.

"Monsieur, Nichols?"

"Yes?"

"We represent Henri's de Montmartre. I think you may know what we wish to discuss."

Fuck yes. Not surprising, but I wasn't prepared for them this soon. Might as well get it over with so I invited them in. A Charles Montlieur from the Company, and a Jacque Laudrau from a law firm.

I let them in but did not invite them to sit down. Laudrau began, "Mister. Nichols, did you provide the Daily Mirror or other publications with comments about Parfum de Femme?"

"Get to the point Monsieur Landrau," I responded sharply.

"Very well, Mister Nichols, the 'point' as you say, is that we believe you have provided certain media with allegations as to the design of our Henri's de Montmartre's Parfum de Femme that are maliciously designed to damage the company. If you continue this in any further way, the Company will have no other option than to seek civil and maybe even criminal action against you."

"And you think it was me because you know I invented it?"

Both lawyers looked at each other with a slight expression of puzzlement. Landrau responded, "We do not know about that, Mister Nichols, but we do know that you were employed by Henri's de Montmartre in a capacity where you would have access to sensitive company designs."

You have to hate lawyers. Bad enough about the injustices of the law, the power of money, but it's the fact that you are talking to a hired gun. Their whole objective is to win as much as possible for their client and to hell with you. By definition they are employed as an advocate of their client. There's no such thing as doing business with them.

"Sounds like you're threatening me, Jack. Problem is it's true. Parfum de Femme has its origins in a pig's pussy. The science can validate it. The House of Henri's de Montmartre is fucked."

"Not necessarily, Mister Nichols," Landrau said, unphased by my comments. "Tabloid stories are frequently false and ridiculous. The Company can possibly stop the damage you have started. If you cease now the Company will not pursue legal action."

"Listen you assholes, you tell the Company they fucked me, now it's my turn. You won't sue me. Do you think the Company wants evidence to come out in court as to where their magnificent product came from?"

Montlieur spoke for the first time. "That would be unwise, Mister Nichols. Do you have any idea the amount of money that is at stake here? Do you think the Company will not do everything possible to stop you?"

"That certainly sounds like a threat."

"It is, Mister Nichols. I suggest you choose wisely."

Landrau threatened legal action. Montlieur was possibly suggesting something else. Landrau appeared concerned.

"Consider this, Mister Nichols. The Company might be willing to compensate you for preventing any further negative publicity. Ultimately this is just a business problem."

"Not to me it isn't. The Company screws me out of recognizing my work. They fire me. You threaten me with being sued. Montlieur suggests perhaps something more. Now you want to pay me off. The Company is a bunch of assholes and you guys are whores. Get the fuck out of here."

Landrau sighed as he left. Montlieur gave me a menacing look.

I should have got the message. Since I did not, a stronger form was delivered a few days later.

It was Friday. I had just finished dinner with a girl named Julie. It was our second date. She worked at the soap company in Accounting. The night was warm but a little drizzle was coming down. Typical Parisian atmosphere. Great for a walk, with a little wine and the prospects of making love.

We were strolling along a back street south of the Rue de Saint Germain when two large men came up behind and pressed a gun into my back. The other guy grabbed Julie and threatened her with a long-bladed knife. We were pushed down an alley well back off the street. One man held Julie against a wall by the throat. The other guy hit me hard in the stomach.

I went down on my knees and vomited as waves of pain swept over me.

"We were told to make you understand what happens if you continue to make trouble," the man said in English with a heavy French accent. "Watch."

The man holding Julie said to her, "If you make any noise I'll cut you."

He proceeded to slice her knit dress down the front from the neck to the hem. The dress gaped open revealing bra and panties. He first cut the bra. His gloved hands roughly grabbed a breast. Julie's slight cry of pain was cut short by the sight of the knife held under her eye. One hand pulled her panties away from her stomach and with the other the man sliced through the fabric with the knife.

"You like this girl, monsieur? Is she good to you in bed? You like her pussy? I think that you would not like me to cut up her pussy, no?"

I looked up to see him lay the knife blade flat against her pubic hair. I gasped. Julie let out a terrified but slight sound as she felt the cool of the steel. The guy with the knife laughed. "Next time I will make no man want her."

The man turned to Julie and took in the full sight of her exposed body, still with the knife to her face.

"There will be no other warnings," the other guy who had hit me said. Then he kicked me in the midsection.

Several minutes later I pulled myself together. Julie was sitting on the ground, her coat pulled around her. She was sobbing. When I went to touch her she thrashed out with her fists at me. She screamed at me in French, "Don't touch me! What did you do to cause that? Is this some drug thing?"

I eventually got her up and we left the alley. I hailed a cab and told him to take us to the nearest police station. That was another mistake.

I was there all night. After an initial conversation, Julie was lead away by a female officer. I'm sure they thought this might be about a rape. A few hours later, the questions seemed to be directed towards drugs. Julie's speculations no doubt. My story, the true story was obviously not believed. These gendarmes were not about to open an investigation against Henri's de Montmartre based on a young American's allegations. Especially since that American was admittedly fired by Henri's, had drank a couple bottles of wine, and was with a hysterical woman with her clothing cut away.

I should have been more scared. There was too much money at stake. Instead, I was so enraged that I was actually calm. No question about what to do. The total destruction of Henri's de Montmartre was a righteous cause.

I never saw Julie again. She would not take my calls. I eventually sent her flowers and a note. I never saw the soap company again either. My boss was a good guy. I called him and told him my parents had been killed in an accident and I would have to resign and return to the U.S. A lot easier story than the truth.

I immediately made arrangements to leave France. My thirty-day deal with the Daily Mirror was up. I was going to stick a hot poker up Henri's de Montmartre's asshole. The best place was the U.S. newspapers and trades. Besides, there was good reason not to make it easier for hired thugs to find me.

I found a modest hotel in New York. Not my favorite city but it was the center of the media and fashion trades. After a week I was able to arrange an interview with a trade publication and the New York Times Fashion editor.

The trade publication woman wasn't buying any part of my story. It wasn't about fashion. She wasn't interested about news. This was just another tabloid story. The meeting with the Times was different.

Joanna Blaine, the fashion editor saw the bigger story. During our meeting she called in reporters for both regular news and business. We spent several hours together. They would check me out and let me know. Which they did three days later. The story ran the following week. It got a brief play on page one and a pretty good article in the Business Section. Over the course of the next couple of weeks, it grew in the Business Section, eventually getting back on page one as a story of some significance. The wire services had picked it up. Other major dailies and the weekly business magazines started running articles. Henri's public relations people could not deflect the tsunami of a shitstorm that continued to build momentum.

The reversal in sales revenues was staggering. Parfum de Femme had been a blockbuster product that was now crashing and burning. It still did what it did for the male libido but women intuitively did not want to splash themselves with what was being incorrectly characterized as an excretion from a pig's vagina. The Company executives had started out with vigorous denials but had now circled the wagons, responding only with terse press releases.

Worse than the lost profits was the damage to the image of Henri's de Montmartre. Worse yet was the eighty percent drop in stock value. The financial community rumored about insolvency and potential sale of the eighty year old firm.

By now, regular newspapers were postmorteming the demise of the great fashion company. U.S. tabloids continued to expand the story with bizarre concepts. Fine with me. After setting their thugs on Julie and me, watching Henri's de Montmartre self-destruct was pure satisfaction.

After three weeks I was out of New York. Bound for an interview. In Milan, Italy, no less. La Casa di Medici, the Italian counterpart fashion firm to Henri's was interested in my perfume concept. The head of North American marketing interviewed me. I gave him the whole story. Told him I believed I could create the same aphrodisiac effects inorganically. No pigs or other negative marketing sources. I was not as confident as I portrayed.

But the easiest sell is to a salesman. Told him I could circumvent Henri's patent. I would need time, a lab, and
resources. I would need a job.

In less than a week I was back on a plane to Italy. La
Casa di Medici was located on the Via Sant'Andrea in the
so-called Quadrilatero, the heart of the Italian fashion
industry. Giorgio Armani and Trussardi shared the same
street. I gave the same pitch to the managing director.
What clinched it was his witnessing my back and forth
exchange with the director of product development.
Good guy. Talented guy. Not anything like Vallot. We
got into a real deep technical discussion. I did have a
solid idea and even their chief technical guy got interested about the possibilities.

I was offered a position on the spot. Two days later I
started at the lab. Unfortunately not in the upscale Quadrilatero district, but in a nondescript building in an industrial complex. The Company found me a prized
apartment in a quiet, upscale neighborhood, obviously
pulling some strings.

Milan is a great city but you could not prove it by me
in my first few months there. It is not beautiful like the
other great cities of Italy such as Rome, Venice, or Flor-
ence. But it is chic. It is at the heart of the Italian economy
and it's the center of fashion.

My fifteen-hour days did pay off. My theories were
correct. With the collaboration of my boss Vittorio, we
not only duplicated the success of Parfum de Femme, but
also improved its aphrodisiac effects. And the fragrance
was superior.

Somewhere during my intense work I found the opportunity to get a new girlfriend. I found Angelina in the
information system department of my new company.
Same way Dominique and I got together. Both were dark
haired beauties, but Angelina was different. Where Do-

minique was mercurial, Angelina was calmer and more thoughtful.

Angelina was every bit the lover that Dominique had been. I asked her one night after lovemaking, "Have you ever heard of the French perfume Parfum de Femme?"

"Of course. Everyone has. Why do you ask?" She said a little defensively.

"Ever use it?"

"Mark, why are you asking me this?"

"Angelina, did you use it, and did men react?"

Angelina looked hard at me with an uncertain expression, not knowing what she should say. "Why do you ask me this, Mark?"

"Because I know something of this perfume."

"So do I. It came from pigs."

"Well not exactly. But it worked didn't it?"

Angelina smiled coyly. "Yes."

"Try this." I gave her a small, unlabelled vial.

She opened the stopper and sniffed carefully. "Smells nice." She dabbed some behind her ears and on her throat."

I kissed her and drank in the scent. The effect was subtle but decidedly there. "I hope a lot of women like it. It's my new creation. I think this time I'll make a lot of money." And make a lot of love.

Like an old joke said about sex, 'If you could bottle it, you'd make a fortune.' Well, I did bottle it.

THE END

By Douglas Clark

"Cry 'Havoc!' and let slip the dogs of war."
William Shakespeare, Julius Caesar III.i

Day one, Tuesday 2:08AM, White House Oval Office, Washington, D.C.

Everyone rose as the President entered the Oval Office.

"Be seated gentlemen," President Frederick Long said. The President was dressed in casual slacks and a sweater. "Who wants to start?"

Helen Gladding, the National Security Advisor, responded immediately, "The best we can tell at this time is that a large commercial jet, probably a Boeing 757, crashed into the Indian Parliament building at approximately 2:15 pm. The aircraft apparently was an Air India flight that had taken off from Bombay. The plane was off course, no reported emergency. Air traffic control was not able to establish contact before the crash."

"Are you saying it was a hijacking.......a 9/11 type of attack?" The President asked.

"We can't be certain at this time, Mister President, but it can't be ruled out."

"Christ Almighty. If this is a Muslim suicide thing, all hell will come down. How many dead?"

"Not determined yet, but it's bad. We think that a large number of the Indian Parliament perished," Gladding responded.

An aide entered the Oval Office and handed a message to the President's Chief of Staff, Samuel Tully.

After reading the message, Tully took a deep, audible breath and said, "Helen was right. Most of the Parliament were killed, or are still missing. But that's not the worst of it. There's someone claiming credit for this as an attack. There are reports on TV now."

Someone turned on the television. A reporter was saying, '.... you can hear the sirens and see the smoke from the Parliament building which is about four blocks from where I am standing. To repeat this breaking news, what we believe to be a Boeing 727, of Air India flight 98 originating out of Bombay, was possibly hijacked and flown deliberately into the Indian Parliament building. Approximately one hour ago, a taped message was delivered to a local New Delhi radio station purportedly from a group calling themselves Allah's Servants. The group claims Islamic religious sovereignty over the disputed Kashmir region, the source of continual armed conflict between India and Pakistan. An un-named Indian police official suggests that casualties will run into the hundreds of dead and wounded. The Prime Minister was not in the building at the time of the crash and he has declared a national state of emergency.'

Chief of Staff Sam Tully muted the television.

"Who do we have missing right now, Sam?" The President asked, meaning which senior staff were absent from Washington at the moment.

"Secretary Smith and Director Claridge are in Paris. They will be at our embassy within the hour. Under Secretary Fielding is here representing State and Deputy Director of Intelligence Kolinski for the CIA. Clyde will be here any minute. He's prepping his press relations staff for the expected barrage from the media. The Vice President of course is in Japan. He's been contacted and is making his way to the U.S. Embassy in Tokyo."

"Senior military commanders are assembling in the Pentagon Situation Room as we speak, Mister President. Assistant Secretary Williams is also there," Secretary of Defense Jonathan Mueller said.

"Suggestions on where we start?" The President asked.

"I suggest that you personally call Prime Minister Singh, Mister President. Give him assurances about U.S. support. The Indians are going to be hell-bent to leave the reservation and do something in Kashmir. They need to feel our support, but also our weight," Secretary Mueller said.

"And how should we make our weight felt, Mister Secretary? Threaten military action in response to their own 9/11? Sanctions?" Under Secretary of State Carter Fielding said, directing his comments to the Defense Secretary.

The exchange pointed to the fundamental riff between State and Defense, on philosophical, strategic, and even tactical approaches to foreign policy. The Defense Secretary himself enjoyed unparalleled influence with the White House allowing for encroachment into State's sphere of influence. More broadly, it was this administration's political appointees forming a solid, coordinated, and activist leadership against the career staff of both Defense and State. The generals at the Pentagon were having just as tough a time as the senior staffers at the State Department.

On a personal level, Fielding saw Secretary Mueller as the ideological head of what was known as the 'Lone Star' government amongst its detractors. Most, including the President were either Texans or heavily connected to Texas business. The senior staff in the Administration were chronically insular in their decision making. To Fielding, they were dangerously arrogant and saw world issues in simplistic concepts. They were victims of the 'group-think syndrome', where the collective opinions of like-minded people create fact out of hypothesis.

Fielding had spent the last several years as a senior diplomat negotiating the highest priority situations for the United States. He held dual doctorates in political science and history. He was a career staffer with eighteen years at the State Department. After the last two years under this administration, he was close to resigning.

"We need to plant the idea in the Indian government that any reactionary escalation of military hostilities in Kashmir will be contrary to their interests. And that there are inducements to avoid such adventures. Small carrots, but a large stick," Mueller responded, but directed his comments to the President, not to Fielding.

Fielding and Mueller had tangled on more than one occasion.

"We should advise Singh that we would apply all pressure to Pakistan to crush these terrorist groups in Kashmir. We will halt military aid until there are concrete results in that effort. In turn, we will accelerate military sales to India. All of course if India shows restraint," Mueller added.

"Mister Fielding, your advice?" The President said.

"Secretary Mueller's approach will not work. India and Pakistan almost went to war not that long ago over lesser provocations than this. Mister President, their parliament has been destroyed. Prime Minister Singh must respond in some strong manner, or his government, what's left of it, will fall. At this point we may even have an issue of the Indian military pushing its own agenda, similar to the Pakistani situation," Fielding answered.

"Fine, then what do you recommend?" The President asked abruptly.

"Call Prime Minister Singh. Get a feel for what direction he might be pursuing. Offer our direct efforts in seeking to identify and destroying the terrorists that caused this."

"In what form might those direct efforts take, Mister Fielding?" Mueller asked. "You're not suggesting we offer to send military forces into Kashmir are you?"

"Like Afghanistan you mean?" Fielding answered sarcastically. "How do we justify threatening India into not responding in the same manner as the U.S. did?"

"Christ, the problem with you intellectuals is that there are endless viewpoints, endless options, and endless discussions. We need to prevent India and Pakistan from getting out of hand."

"I don't think that you---"

"Gentlemen, enough wrangling," the President interrupted. "What do we do next? Other opinions?"

Chief of Staff Tully said, "I think you should get Prime Minister Singh on the telephone immediately, Sir. Condolences of course, but as Jonathan said, make it known that the U.S. cannot accept any response into Kashmir that could escalate into war with Pakistan. I would also suggest we get out in front on this thing, Call a news conference here at seven. Make the morning news as people are getting ready for work. Express outrage.

Pledge support on the continuing global war on terror. Give assurances to India. Caution against ill-considered military action. Clyde's people can put it together in the next couple of hours."

"Get it in the works, Sam. Get the call into the Prime Minister."

There was continued discussion in the Oval Office for the next twenty minutes until the call went through to Prime Minister Singh. The President put the call on the speaker.

"Prime Minister Singh. The people of the United States wish to express our condolences and grief over this attack on your government. We know only too well the depth of your loss."

"Thank you, Mister President. Terrorism is not new to India. However, this act has reached a new level. At least two-thirds of the members of Parliament were killed or wounded. Our intelligence people know the group that has taken credit. Not only have they taken credit, but they have also advertised the names of the perpetrators. The leader, the pilot of the aircraft was a former Pakistani air force pilot. His name is known to our intelligence people."

"Prime Minister Singh, it is particularly important that the government of India exercise restraint in their response to this attack. The government of the United States will do everything in its power to assist India in this terrible time, and it will use its influence and resources to bring this terrorist group to justice," President Long said.

There was a long pause before Prime Minister Singh answered. "Mister President, if you will forgive me for sounding ungrateful, there is little of substance the United States can offer. Unless you are offering to participate in resolving the long-standing sponsorship of terrorists by Pakistan."

President Long responded, "I realize that the history of the Kashmir region has been difficult for a long time. However, the world cannot afford to have India and Pakistan at war. My intelligence people assure me that there is no government sponsorship of terrorist groups by the government of Pakistan."

"I beg to differ with you, Mister President. My intelligence people have for some time obtained proof of direct financing from Pakistani government agencies, and particularly their military. Known terrorists are harbored in Pakistan. There is direct military training and equipping of Kashmir terrorist groups. This latest attack has the marks of planning that would be beyond what this organization is capable of. It is the same as Syria's sponsorship of Palestinian terrorists."

"Again, Mister Prime Minister, I urge restraint. I understand you have declared a state of emergency and placed your military forces on high alert status. I am told that President Ansar has responded with a similar order to Pakistani forces. This could easily escalate beyond anyone's control."

"What would you have me do, Mister President? If I practice, as you call it, restraint, this government will fall. Perhaps you fail to grasp the reality that the political leadership, both the governing coalition and the opposition's has largely been murdered. If I were to do nothing, in all probability the military would take charge. That aside, Mister President, I am personally committed to see this attack redressed, and to settle the Kashmir issue with finality."

"Again, Mister Prime Minister, I must warn against military action –"

Singh interrupted the President, "Restraint? Are you suggesting that the United States is threatening India if it exercises its right to defend itself? Can only the United States take military action against its enemies? Must other states of the world seek permission of the United States?"

"Mister Prime Minister, at the least, we urge India to take this before the Security Council. The United States will take the lead in pushing for action."

Even through Singh's precise British accent, one could sense his seething anger. "What would the United States do? Press for sanctions against Pakistan? Not very likely in view of your closeness in support of chasing terrorists important only to the United States. Would the United States use its military forces to destroy terrorists in Kashmir? Not at all likely I should think?"

"Mister President, India will protect its sovereignty with all means at its disposal. The decades of Pakistan's sponsorship of terrorist against the State of India will end from here on out. It will be ended." Prime Minister Singh said.

"That sounds like a declaration of war, Mister Prime Minister."

"You could infer that. I believe there is nothing further to discuss, Mister President." The Indian Prime Minister disconnected.

"That sonofabitch hung up on me. Backward, second-rate country," the President said. "The issue is the nukes. What's the situation there, Helen?"

Helen Gladding was in her early fifties, somewhat matronly in appearance. She tended toward gray suits and little make-up. The requisite doctorate in political science did not temper her use of strong language. While not as acerbic as the Defense Secretary, she was essentially the opposite gender equivalent. Although from Missouri, she fit into the Texas style nicely.

"The latest information, correct me if I am wrong, Dan, is that India has perhaps as many as twenty devices, probably all between ten and twenty kilotons yields,"

Gladding said. "Single stage fission only. No second stage thermonuclear devices."

"How big is that?" President Long asked.

"Roughly the same yield range as those dropped on Hiroshima and Nagasaki."

"And the Pakistanis?"

"We think less number of devices. Probably no more than ten. Might not be as large in yields as the Indians," Gladding answered.

"What do we think the Indians will do?" President Long asked.

There was a long silence before anyone spoke.

Defense Secretary Mueller was the first to voice an opinion. "There's no way to know what the Indians intend. Singh probably doesn't even know yet. He'll assemble his generals and plan some sort of military action. That is reasonably certain. What's more important is that we prevent it from getting out of hand. We can't let these two third world countries let the nuclear genie out of the bottle. If we have to lean on either or both real hard, so be it."

Mueller was warming to the scenario. "I would recommend an immediate ordering of at least two carrier battle groups to move into the northern Arabian Sea off the coast of Pakistan. We have four groups currently in the Middle East. We can move the two groups from the Persian Gulf and be on station in perhaps forty-eight hours."

"I agree with Jonathan," Helen Gladding said. "We must control this situation. We need time and maybe a large projection of U.S. force will cause the Indians to consider matters more broadly."

"We can take a strong demanding posture that puts a heavy hammer to the Pakistanis, and at the same time make the Indians think about any military action. It puts

teeth in your caution to Singh that the world will not tolerate an Indian-Pakistani war," Mueller said.

"I think at the least we can expect a major offensive
by the Indians in the Kashmir," Fielding said. "The Pakistanis will of course respond. There will most assuredly
be a war. Singh may even declare war on Pakistan very
soon. On this I think the U.S. cannot effectively be the
unilateral instrument of containing the Indians and Pakistanis. The Chinese will be the key, but we also need the
Europeans with us on this. In fact, Mister President, I
would recommend you begin calling each of the key
heads-of-state, starting with Premier Lei."

"Jesus Christ, Fielding. You'd have us diddling with
these interminable diplomatic debates while Rome, or
more realistically, Karachi and New Delhi burn. You of
all people should understand the use of force. It was your
white paper that suggested that extreme *nuclear hammer*
approach," Mueller said.

"What are you referring to, Jonathan?" The President
asked.

"Mister Fielding authored a State Department white
paper several years ago that advocated the use of nuclear
retaliatory force on any country that used a nuclear device on another state. Interesting concept, but not diplo-
matically realistic," Mueller answered.

"Why the change of thinking now on this present
problem, Doctor Fielding?" The President asked.

Mueller's characterization of Fielding's paper omitted
several key elements, which Fielding explained to the
President. His plan called for a declaration that the
United States holds the fundamental proposition that the
use of a nuclear device by any state against another state
would be construed as directly threatening the security of
the United States. Therefore, the United States would declare that if any state were to use a nuclear weapon, that
state would suffer complete annihilation from the United

States as a matter of self-defense. In essence, it resurrected the Cold War concept of assured self-destruction as a deterrent to initiating nuclear conflict.

Fielding's plan called for making the attempt to recruit the principle nuclear powers of the United Kingdom, France, Russia, and China to the treaty. He argued that apart from the British, the other powers would not join in any such treaty, and would condemn the U.S. for such an attempt to coerce the rest of the world. The plan was to cause a heated worldwide debate, that in the end left the United States no alternative but to independently declare its threat.

The result would be increased leverage against countries with nuclear weapons programs, and potentially a real deterrent. If actual retaliation was ever necessary, the argument had already been made. The offending country duly warned. Much of the world might lobby and protest, but the debate would already be history, a policy of long standing by the time it might have to be invoked.

In the end, the previous President did not feel he had the political capital to risk such a bold stroke. Fielding's paper was much discussed by foreign policy wonks. The Secretary of State never championed the move. The concept was buried.

"Hell of a concept, Doctor. Truly Machiavellian. Makes you out as more of a hawk than even Jonathan here," the President said. "Why not make a threat now to both the Indians and Pakistanis? What's the difference if we had done it some time ago?"

The President was more intellectually shallow and unknowledgeable than Fielding had thought. He had no grasp of the fundamental strengths that accrued from a standing policy as opposed to a reactionary response. Nobody else in the previous Administration did either. Like the Dr. Strangelove character in the movie commenting on the Soviet's doomsday machine: *It loses its meaning if it's not made public!*

Fielding answered in a more challenging tone than he intended, "If they resorted to a nuclear exchange, would you be willing to retaliate with a U.S. nuclear strike, Sir?"

"You can't expect the President to answer such a question, Doctor," Mueller interjected.

Fielding ignored Mueller and addressed the President. "My point, Mister President, is that, had it been our avowed policy, then you could invoke such a threat with real teeth, and without invoking a new international debate."

"It wouldn't be a debate, Doctor. We wouldn't take it to the U.N., and go through another Iraq debacle. We'd just do it," Secretary Mueller said.

Chief of Staff Tully interrupted the exchange. "Mister President, Admiral O'Brien just called and advised that satellite data is picking up what appears to be a large-scale military deployment by India. We should move to the Situation Room so we can see what the Pentagon sees, Sir."

The Oval Office emptied and followed the President to the elevator to descend to the secure White House Situation Room. They were followed by an air force major with an attaché case manacled to his wrist. The attaché case was the "football", code name for the presidential nuclear authentication codes system.

Day one, Tuesday 5:55 AM, White House Situation Room, Washington, D.C.

Three Marine sergeants were stationed outside as the elevator opened. Upon entering through heavy doors, one looked upon the opposite wall of the large room with its fifty-foot curved wall covered in over-sized panels of specially designed high definition monitors. Arrayed in a corresponding arc was a high-tech conference-like table with seating for twenty people. Each position had its own electronic and voice communications, and an angled monitor under the glass top. Manning the sophisticated electronics was a team of five military officers. The room had gone through a total technological upgrade each decade or so since the early sixties.

Everyone took a seat after the President.

"Get Admiral O'Brien on the phone," the President ordered.

On the 'phone' was actually a secure data line that brought the Admiral into full view on one of the monitors. By voice activation, when anyone spoke from either the Pentagon's or the White House Situation Room, that person's face would appear on screen. If multiple people spoke, the screen split to display as many as necessary.

The President addressed The Chairman of the Joints Chiefs of Staff, Admiral Clarence O'Brien. "Admiral, tell us what's going on."

"These are real-time satellite photos of heavy military traffic moving north up the A1 Highway from the city of Jammu." The huge wall monitors displayed the photos.

"We estimate two full divisions may be in transit. This is essentially their reserve force supporting forward positions north of Strinagar. They would typically be in a high state of readiness. We can probably expect other elements of the Indian Army to start moving soon to replace these two divisions. I am told it would take a couple of days to mobilize that much transport, a few more to move very large numbers of troops," Admiral O'Brien said.

"Mister President, this is General Brewster. The Indian Air Force has gone to their equivalent of a war footing alert. We are already seeing increased patrols not only in Kashmir, but along the Pakistan border to the south near the city of Lahore." General Richard Brewster was Chief of Staff of the Air Force.

"So what's this mean?" the President asked.

"It means that Prime Minister Singh is saber rattling. He's got to in the face of this attack on their parliament," Secretary Mueller said.

"I think it can and will go way beyond saber rattling, Mister President," Carter Fielding said. "I think that the Indians will take a heavy hand to crush militant Muslim groups in Kashmir. I would expect them to attack the Pakistan Army in the Kashmir region."

"Mister Fielding, the Indians and Pakistanis will come to some level of blows. They always do. They've been doing it for fifty years. The Pakistanis didn't launch an attack on the Indian Parliament. Beyond the Indian rhetoric, they know that it's extremist terrorist groups. There is no serious evidence that the Pakistani government sponsors, or even supports these groups," Mueller said.

"Mister President, we need to get Secretary Fuller's read on this. No offense to Mister Fielding, but Tim has a strong background in the sub-continent," Mueller said.

Timothy Fuller was Secretary of State, a former general and commander of NATO. His *background* in the sub-continent consisted solely of a former position as commander of the U.S. Central Command, where Indian and Pakistan were within that sphere of operations. Secretary Fuller was in Europe and expected to join the discussions via telephone soon from the U.S. Embassy in Zurich.

"We're expecting to get Secretary Fuller in secure communications contact very soon, Mister President," Sam Tully said.

One member at the table was speaking in hushed tones into a telephone, "Christ – are we sure? What do we have to corroborate?" There was a pause before he responded, "Very well, you'll stand by this? I'll be passing it on to the Boss?" He hung up the telephone.

"Mister President, we have some troubling developments," Daniel Kolinski, Deputy Director of Central Intelligence said. "It appears that the Indians may be deploying their nuclear weapons."

"My God. Dan, how do we know that?" Helen Gladding asked.

"We have had an asset in place inside the Indian military for a number of years. He's a mid-rank officer in their air force. We just received word through his control in Kanpur that three warheads are being moved for assembly into operational weapons." CIA Deputy Director Kolinski said.

"How long before they could be operational, Dan?" Mueller asked.

"Within twenty-four hours."

"What can we do to stop them?" The President asked.

There were several moments of silence. Several people looked at each other. Helen Gladding finally spoke up.

"We need to up the pressure on Singh. Tell him we are aware of his potential deployment of nuclear weapons. Tell him of the dire consequences if he goes forward. Give him an alternative."

"Like what?" the President asked.

"Strong U.S. intervention on their side. Leaning heavily on the Pakistanis. Forcing their support to clamp down on terrorist groups. Increased military support. Direct U.S. commitment to resolving the Kashmir question," Mueller responded. "Perhaps suggesting U.S. support based upon treating Kashmir in the same way as Afghanistan; as a breeding ground for terrorism. Fair game for the U.S. to partner with India with direct military intervention. Then again, Mister President, we could consider taking a page out of Doctor Fielding's approach.

Threaten that any use of nuclear weapons would require a nuclear response from the United States in the interest of its own security."

"Hardly the same circumstance since we didn't make that our previous standing policy," Fielding said. "Do you believe that India would take seriously any U.S. threat to attack them if they were to use a nuclear device? Dan, what's the intelligence on the Pakistanis?"

"We know they have gone to a high alert status. Satellite intel points to the start of troop movements towards the border," Dan Kolinski answered.

"The missiles?" Fielding asked.

Kolinski hesitated before answering. The CIA had comparatively poor intelligence from inside Pakistan as with most Muslim countries. Reliance was more heavily based on technological intelligence, satellite photographs and communications intercepts, rather than human assets. The missiles Fielding was asking about were mobile, visible from satellite imaging, but difficult to monitor in real time and easily camouflaged. While the Indians would rely on aircraft as their means of delivering a nuclear warhead, the Pakistanis would probably use medium range surface launched ballistic missiles.

Turning from Fielding to the President, Kolinski answered, "It's not certain what the Pakistanis are doing, Mister President. Our people intelligence is more limited."

"Are you saying we don't know their state of missile readiness? Would we know if or when the missiles would be armed with nuclear warheads?" Fielding interjected.

Helen Gladding attempted to defuse Fielding's potential argument. 'We all know that the situation in Pakistan is more difficult, Carter."

"God damnit, Helen, the point is we don't know what the Pakistanis are doing, much less what they might do.

We're speculating about a strategy to contain the Indians and we don't know anything about the situation in Pakistan. What if there is substance to the Indian's allegations about Pakistan's support of this attack on their parliament?"

Dropping any pretext of civility, Mueller said, "Christ, Fielding, what are you suggesting we do? We're trying to defuse a major crisis and you want to open an intellectual debate on the merits and evidence."

"As opposed to reacting half-cocked with our typical unilateral arrogance," Fielding said. He instantly regretted the statement.

The President flushed. "Explain that comment Doctor Fielding."

Fielding took a moment to compose his emotions and to focus on dealing pragmatically with the situation at hand. "Mister President, first of all, there may be substance in India's allegations about Pakistan's complicity. Perhaps not directly, but it is clearly probable that certain elements of President Ansar's government may provide active support to terrorist groups. Groups hostile to the United States I might add. Ansar rules only by a coalition of support. He's a political opportunist that understands his power base."

"Let me understand, Doctor, you are counseling restraint in trying to stop India from going to war with Pakistan, and potentially unleashing a nuclear exchange? Perhaps we should threaten Pakistan instead," Mueller interjected.

"Not exactly, but you're on track, Mister Secretary. We should put equal pressure on Pakistan." Fielding said, and then addressed the President. "I recommend that you contact President Ansar and pressure him equally not to escalate events beyond control."

"No offense, Doctor Fielding, but I don't see all the nuances that you see," The President said. "The problem with you guys at State is that you argue both sides and want to see a negotiated settlement. Our position is to deal strongly with India and put a lid on their response. The Pakistanis will not do anything rash unless provoked by the Indians. It's not a question of right, but of consequences. Once we accomplish that, we can get some breathing room. Why shouldn't the U.S. leverage its power in the interest of world peace?"

The President's last remark seemed rhetorical. Fielding did not continue the debate. A moment of icy silence was broken by Admiral O'Brien calling attention to the video display.

"Mister President, the display symbols you are seeing as indicated by the arrows on the map, show deployment of approximately thirty Pakistani Ghouri missiles fitted to mobile launchers. These are medium range ballistic missiles with a range of 800 miles. The movement is symbolic since twenty or so miles closer to India makes no difference. It would appear that they want to announce to us that they are ready to respond to any level of attack by Indian forces."

"Do we know if they're armed with nuclear warheads, Admiral?"

Admiral O'Brien said, "I would defer to Mister Kolinski for a better opinion on that, but no, we do not, Mister President."

"Probable, Mister Kolinski?"

"I don't know that I would characterize it as probable, but it is certainly possible, Sir," Kolinski answered.

Chief of Staff Tully interrupted, "Mister President, I have messages requesting return calls to various heads-of-state; the U.K., France, Spain, Italy, others, and Premier Lei of China.

The President directed his Chief of Staff to get President Ansar of Pakistan on the telephone first. In the meantime, he suggested everyone take a break and get some coffee.

Fifteen minutes later, after the initial diplomatic niceties were out of the way, President Long directly asked, "What are Pakistan's intentions, Mister President?"

After the translation lag, President Ansar answered, "That appears to be up to the Indian government. This attack was not sponsored by my government. Even if it turns out to be correct that some disaffected ex-military officer participated in this attack, that does not mean my government was behind it. India seems bound to use this as a pretext to a large-scale attack on Pakistan. I must tell you, President Long, that as we speak, Pakistan's Military is preparing to counter any attack by the Indians."

President Ansar was an ex-general whose power base was the Military. He was personally non-religious, but he had to cater to fundamentalist factions due to their strong domestic following. He had been effective in reducing funding to such groups, but largely unable to infiltrate them with his security service. This was regrettable since there was much political capital lost by not being able to provide the West with wanted terrorists.

"It is my earnest hope that Pakistan and India can avoid another war, Mister President."

"That is up to India. They are acting as the aggressor. Pakistan must protect itself."

The back and forth continued in this vain for some minutes. President Long finally raised the subject of concern. "Regardless of the potential for armed conflict with India, Mister President, can I have your assurance that you will not resort to the use of nuclear weapons?"

"I am sorry that I cannot give you that assurance, President Long. Pakistan must reserve the right to use all resources in defense of its sovereignty. If India attacks Pakistani cities, perhaps even invades across our borders, what would you have me do? What would you do, Mister President, in my position?"

"I have communicated with Prime Minister Singh a short time ago. Beyond my sympathy for their loss, I communicated in the strongest terms that the world would not allow for another major Pakistan and India war that could lead to a nuclear exchange."

"And if India were to launch a nuclear attack, what would the United States do, Mister President?"

President Long considered the question and looked about the Situation Room for any help. Secretary Mueller rushed over and whispered into the President's ear.

"I am told by my experts that our satellite and other surveillance technology would provide some warning before the Indian's could launch such an attack," President Long answered. Everyone in the Situation Room knew this was impossible. The Indian's could have bombers over Lahore or Karachi within forty-five minutes. Even if the U.S. had carriers in the Arabian Sea off the coast of both countries, there was no practical way U.S. aircraft could thwart an Indian attack.

"And you would do what, Mister President; have your fighters attack the Indian aircraft? Shoot them down? And if they dropped nuclear bombs on Pakistan, what would you do? Retaliate with nuclear bombs on India? I think not." Ansar's voice rose, "Perhaps take the issue to the United Nations? Condemn India in the Security Council? Sanction them? And what of Pakistan lying in waste? What would the United States offer? And what of the rest of the world, Mister President? What do all of you offer Pakistan if India were to strike?"

"I have indicated that the United States would intervene to preclude that from happening, Mister President."

"I am sorry, Mister President, but my experts say that is not possible. The only ultimate deterrent is our own nuclear arsenal. Mutual destruction after all was the foundation for avoiding nuclear war between the United States and the Soviet Union for decades."

The remainder of the conversation consisted of mutual assurances to stay in close contact as events developed.

Carter Fielding said, "Mister President, I believe this could easily escalate beyond any control. Singh's ruling coalition has become increasingly hostile against Pakistan. It is worse than some years ago when they both made suggestions about using nuclear weapons. With heighten U.S. relations with Pakistan, the Indians feel even more compelled to assert their power. With this attack on the Indian Parliament, Singh must take decisive action."

"We know all that, Doctor. What's your point?" Mueller said.

"My point is this; The Indians will launch an offensive, possibly south of Kashmir, directly into Pakistan. Their troop movements will be more than a show of threat. In all likelihood there will be all-out war. The Pakistanis will get the worst of it, primarily because of Indian's advantage in airpower. Pakistan will be pushed into a corner. State's best analysis thinks their general staff would use nuclear weapons if it were a case of imminent destruction of the country."

"Then what course of action do you suggest, Dr. Fielding?" Helen Gladding asked.

"Get as many world leaders as possible to pressure both sides. Make them understand that if either side were to use nuclear weapons that they would become a pariah state. Threaten charges of crimes against humanity for the leadership and military," Fielding said.

"Mister President, I think we should not rely too much on diplomatic efforts alone. We should order our carriers to the area immediately. We should raise our military alert status and let it be known to both sides. We can move a tactical fighter wing into Kabul. I would also suggest we begin high altitude reconnaissance flights over both countries. In short, we need to scare the shit out of both of them," Mueller said.

While the debate waged, Secretary of State Timothy Fuller and CIA Director Walter Claridge were connected by a secure line within the U.S. embassy in Paris.

"Tim, you want to add anything?" the President asked.

"Carter is right that we need to get everyone to gang up on both the Indians and Pakistanis. I've already had some success with the French and Italians. The British of course are on board. I assume you'll be talking with most heads-of-state over the next couple of hours, Mister President. However, Secretary Mueller is also right. We need to up the military threat to the highest possible level. There needs to be a real element of fear from that direction," Secretary Fuller said.

"I agree as well. Anything to add, Walt?" The President said.

"Nothing further at this time, Mister President. Dan has already communicated the latest intel we have," CIA Director Claridge answered.

"Admiral, get the deployments underway immediately as suggested by Secretary Mueller."

"Yes, Sir. I will keep you advised of the timing and asset options available momentarily, Mister President."

The Admiral explained the deployment of U.S. military assets being brought to bear. The carriers Kennedy and Roosevelt and their combined battle groups with a strength of twenty-six warships would be on station off the coast of Pakistan and India in forty-one hours. This would place one hundred eighty-five attack aircraft within minutes of both countries, along with an array of naval platforms to launch cruise missiles.

The Air Force 14th Bomber Wing with fifteen B1 long-range bombers was already based in Turkey. They had been ordered to battle-ready alert, able to take to the air within thirty minutes. The flying time to targets in Pakistan was two hours, another thirty minutes into India. The Strategic Air Command's 3rd Bomber Wing with their twelve B52s was currently based on the island of Diego Garcia in the Indian Ocean with roughly the same flying time to the region as the B1 bombers. Both aircraft types could remain on-station for extended periods with air-to-air refueling. Both could be armed with the entire repertoire of ordinance in the U.S. arsenal, including the full range of nuclear weapons.

Air Force Chief of Staff Richard Brewster suggested a tactical bomber wing specialized in attacking ground installations be moved to Kabul, Afghanistan. These assets could be used against Pakistani missile launching installations. The Navy would have to contend with any Indian aircraft threat.

Carter Fielding and CIA Deputy Director Daniel Kolinski wound up in the lavatory at the urinals alone.

"You think the Indians and Pakistanis might use nukes. Carter?"

"I think it could easily go that far."

"You think Mueller is wrong about using military threats?"

"Christ, Dan, Mueller and the rest of the President's cracker barrel cronies are arrogantly naïve. They're not dealing with the real question that their position leads to, which is, what would we do if either India or Pakistan resorts to nuclear weapons? I don't think they would attack either country. And India and Pakistan know it. And what targets would we attack anyway? God help us if the President thinks a nuclear retaliation is a viable consideration."

"Your original idea, isn't it, Carter?"

"Jesus, don't you start that argument again."

"Just needling, Carter. But tell me, why have you stayed around if you feel the way you do about this administration?"

Fielding washed his hands and splashed water on his face before answering Kolinski. "I wasn't going to. Resignation letter's in my drawer. I was waiting until Fuller returned from Europe. I would have been out of here. Teaching somewhere or making big bucks at a think tank. And what about you Dan? I don't think you're too fond of this bunch either."

"I'm not, but that's irrelevant. I'm just a spook. A career spook. This administration will eventually be replaced by another. Better or maybe worse. But I still get to influence things. There ain't no other place with this much power floating around. And isn't that why you're at State for these many years? You're seduced by the power like everyone else. We're just all whores for power, Carter. "

"Well, I was getting religion and about to get off the street. Now I'm stuck in this fucking catastrophe."

Kolinski took Fielding by the arm and said earnestly, "Stay in there, Carter. You're at least some sort of sanity to Mueller's recklessness. Fuller is a worthless piece of shit. Glad he's in Europe right now. He's just a shill for the President and Mueller."

Day two, Wednesday 7:20AM, White House Situation Room, Washington, D.C.

The senior officials manning the Situation Room at the White House were all showing signs of fatigue after more than twenty-four hours without sleep. Some were disheveled, others had showered and changed clothes, but the effects of the sustained stress were evident on everyone.

Intelligence reported continued mobilization of military forces from both sides. There had been only modest exchanges of artillery fire in Kashmir throughout the day. It was late evening and dark now on the sub-continent. The day had been full of endless discussions with heads-of-state, foreign ministers, and foreign militaries. Some had optimistic thoughts that perhaps the crisis would not escalate. The realists knew better.

"Oh, Christ. Someone get the President right away," Daniel Kolinski shouted. The President had left a few hours earlier to try to get some sleep. "There's been another attack against India."

Fifteen minutes later the President entered the Situation Room dressed for normal business with a suit and tie. "Everyone sit down. Let's hear it."

Kolinski began to report. "About an hour ago, 7:15 pm local time in the Kashmir city of Jammu, a large explosion heavily damaged Indian Army Headquarters. It appears it was a truck bomb, a very large one. Sources on the ground report it appeared to be a two-and-a-half ton truck that ran through the perimeter gate and crashed into a building when it detonated. Fairly large loss of life we're lead to believe."

"What's the verdict on the casualties at the Parliament building?" The President asked.

Helen Gladding answered, "Three hundred seventy-six confirmed dead, so far. Over three hundred injured."

General Brewster came on the video screen. "Mister President, satellite telemetry and AWAC's radar are showing a large force of Indian aircraft about to cross into Kashmir. They appear to be tactical bombers. We're also seeing a large response by the Pakistani's. They're putting up all the fighter aircraft they can. We estimate maybe fifteen minutes before the Indians engage Pakistani targets."

A large digital map zoomed into the region displaying moving symbols, which Brewster advised were the respective aircraft formations.

There was little conversation as everyone waited for the inevitable confrontation to start. Some walked about, others drank coffee. The fifteen minutes passed slowly.

"Looks like they're hitting artillery positions, Sir. However, some aircraft are continuing eastward. I would guess to attack rear supply installations," General Brewster said.

"What about the Pakistani missiles, General?" Secretary Mueller asked.

"I'm afraid we cannot locate them, Sir."

On the screen everyone saw an aide interrupt General Brewster.

"Mister President, if you will look at the display map we have another development. Note the new symbols displayed below the others with comparatively rapid movement on the screen toward the east."

"What is it, General?" asked the President.

"Missiles, Sir. Pakistani missiles. Launched approximately three minutes ago."

"Targeted where?"

"Just a moment, Sir," General Brewster said. An aide was commenting on papers he just placed in front of the General. "Level of confidence?" Brewster asked the aide.

"Very high, Sir."

"Mister President, according to our computer projections of the telemetry, the missiles are most probably targeted on Bombay and New Delhi."

"Are these nuclear, General?"

"There is no way to know, Mister President."

"How long before they reach these cities?"

"Approximately twenty-five to thirty minutes. New Delhi is closest."

The President rubbed his face with both hands, then through his hair. Holding the bridge of his nose, with his eyes turned down, he asked the convened staff, "Comments and recommendations gentlemen, and ladies?"

No one spoke. After some moments of silence the President raised his head and looked at Secretary Mueller.

Mueller sighed. "Well, Mister, President, the reality is that there is little we can do militarily to stop what appears to be war between India and Pakistan. The issue here is whether one side or the other resorts to nuclear weapons."

Carter Fielding injected, "And if they do, what do we do?"

"Mister President, while this is a time of extreme crisis, it is also a time of unique opportunity. An opportunity to demonstrate the will and resources of the United States to prevent the use of weapons of mass destruction," Secretary Mueller said.

"I'm not sure I understand, Jonathan," the President said.

"If either, or perhaps both India and Pakistan resort to nuclear weapons, it will be only the second time in history. Unlike the Cold War the threat of nuclear annihilation between two super powers does not restrain two minor nuclear powers with limited devices, to use them tactically. After all, both India and Pakistan have only small numbers of nuclear weapons, and those are comparatively low yields. Now is the time to implement Doctor Fielding's strategy of threatened retaliation by the United States. However, where Doctor Fielding would have had us declare such a threat in a hypothetical sense, and incur world condemnation, we now have an immediate threat. We warn both sides now that we will respond against the offending country with U.S. nuclear

weapons. The Free World will support us. Enemy regimes will be given a strong message."

"I'm totally against such a thing, Sir," Fielding said.
"My concept was to act as a deterrent against *before* any
initial use. If those Pakistani missiles have nuclear warheads, it would be a compounding disaster for the U.S. to
retaliate with nuclear force against them. Threatening the
use of U.S. nuclear weapons against the Indians to en-
force abstinence on their part not to retaliate with their
own nuclear weapons, will absolutely declare us as a unilateral, dominating power. It will have worse consequences for us, and may not even deter states like North
Korea and Iran. China will become justifiably paranoid."

Turning to address Secretary Mueller, Fielding said,
"Furthermore, it won't work, Mister Secretary. If one side
should use a nuclear device, the other side will be forced
to respond in kind, for political if not cultural reasons.
They will not wait for us. Are we then to bomb them as
well? Besides, are we really prepared to carry through
with a U.S. threat?"

"Are we, Jonathan?" the President asked.

"Yes, Mister President, I think we should be. If India
or Pakistan were to use nuclear weapons without suffering consequences, then we would have real problems. If
we take dominating action, we would have western de-
mocracies on our side. Enemy regimes would be given
the strongest of signals as to our resolve. And, it would
serve to re-establish some of the Hiroshima and Nagasaki
deterrent effect," Mueller answered.

Mueller continued the lecture. "The United States and
the Soviet Union did not use nuclear weapons over four
decades, even while waging wars that could not be won
with conventional weapons. The Indians and Pakistanis
do not have the same fear of mutual destruction. They
simply do not have enough megatons to threaten the
other with mutual annihilation. No matter how horrific,

this is not a doomsday scenario for them. Only the U.S. can impose that threat."

"But to order a nuclear strike when we are not ourselves being attacked, Jonathan. I'm uncomfortable with that," the President said. "What's everybody else's position on this?"

General Brewster, "Mister President, the Indian's have now penetrated Pakistani air space. There's a heavy amount of SAM launches, and air-to-air exchanges. The Indians are striking what appear to be military targets in the Kashmir region."

Brewster was distracted by an aide. Then turned back to address the President. "Sir, it appears that a squadron of bombers with fighter escorts is moving beyond Kashmir. On their present course, it would appear they're headed for Islamabad. We'll know in about twenty minutes. About the same time the Pakistani missiles reach their targets in India."

Satellite intelligence indicated four warheads each were headed for New Delhi and Bombay.

In the intervening minutes, reports indicated that key government buildings in Islamabad, the Pakistan capital, were being heavily bombed. A second and larger group of Indian bombers was being tracked in route from the southeast. Indian ground forces were engaging Pakistani forces with success in Kashmir after destroying significant elements of Pakistani artillery through air attacks.

At 1640 GMT, the twenty-first century was defined as no other century before it.

General Brewster said in a calm voice, "Mother of God. The assholes really did it."

"General? What is it?" The President asked.

"The goddamn Pakistani missiles were nuclear, Mister President. At least a couple were."

Everyone started to yell questions at the same time. Most of the staff picked up telephones.

Defense Secretary Mueller eventually got everyone's attention. "Mister President, we must stop the Pakistanis. They are now a pariah state. They must be crushed with all the might of the United States. This must not be left to political debate. Other states must be made to see the consequences of using a nuclear option. The first of which, Mister President, is India. You must call Prime Minister Singh. He must not retaliate in kind."

From the Pentagon, General Brewster interrupted, "If everyone will turn their attention to the display board. We have zoomed in on Islamabad in tight detail and switched to real-time optical imagery from a high altitude surveillance aircraft. The second wave of Indian bombers should be over Islamabad in two minutes."

Everyone was silent at the White House and Pentagon Situation Rooms. Like a theater with a suspense thriller showing. With no sound, the event was even more chilling.

At 1710 GMT, an enormous explosion appeared on the screen. Everyone had seen this event previously on film; Trinity, Hiroshima, and Nagasaki in 1945.

"Mute question now about leaning on the Indians. Or do you propose we bomb the shit out of both of them, Mister Secretary?" Fielding said in anger and disgust directed at the Secretary of Defense.

Like everyone else, Fielding was at his emotional breaking point. Without any real sleep for the last thirty-six hours, he did not care much if he kept his emotions in check. Why the hell had he stayed around so long with these people? Now he was at the seat of power, yet everyone here was powerless to stop the world from sliding into chaos. All the artifacts of modern political science were just academic exercises.

"Not quite that indiscriminate, Doctor. However, I would........"

Chief of Staff Tully rushed over to the President who was sweating profusely and in obvious distress.

"Call a doctor!" Tully yelled. Something serious was happening. Several people helped Tully ease the President to the floor. Someone loosen his tie and placed a rolled up suit jacket under his head.

The President was unconscious when a doctor arrived five minutes later. The doctor started CPR. EMTs arrived minutes later. They used a defibrillator.

"Helicopter will be here in two minutes," an aide yelled.

The President left on a gurney.

An army major with the 'football', the metal briefcase with the nuclear launch code authority, followed the gurney.

"Fielding, where the hell's Benson?" Daniel Kolinski asked in a hushed tone. John Benson was Vice President of the United States.

Day three, Thursday, 2:20 AM, White House Situation Room, Washington, D.C.

The President never regained consciousness.

Returning from Japan, Air Force Two stopped in Chicago to pick up a federal judge. Vice President John Benson was sworn in as President before landing in Washington.

Vice President Benson was not so much a shallow thinker as he was a single minded one that viewed issues with blinders for anything that might conflict with his views. Politically savvy, but easily manipulated, he got to the ticket as a three term Michigan governor that brought in Midwest votes. He was excluded from the White House inner circle. Now it was time to pay the piper.

Benson was neither emotionally or intellectually prepared for the Presidency. He arrived at the White House

Situation Room at 3:30 am. He was uncharacteristically disheveled with a look of bewilderment.

His Chief of Staff ushered him into his chair.

"My God. Can someone please bring me up to speed?" The new President asked.

Everyone looked to Secretary of Defense Mueller. The outspoken hawk of the Administration, and its most prominent foreign policy force did not immediately respond to his new President's request. After an uncomfortable silence, Carter Fielding took the initiative and went over the sequence of events.

Upon Fielding's conclusion, Benson closed his eyes, "Thank you, Doctor Fielding. Can you explain what options we have?"

Carter Fielding was awash with emotions and thoughts. There were no clear actions. Frankly, he did not know what the hell to recommend.

Fielding started to respond, "Mister, President, there are no clear options for the United States unilaterally. The first order of business is to contact other heads-of-state and ...."

"Mister President, we have a new development," Admiral O'Brien said. "Something is going on in Israel. We have a number of intelligence reports of some sort of massive civil disorder occurring. Unfortunately, we have no verifiable details. The Israeli military has gone to high alert. Neither Defense nor State is able to get through to anyone of rank in the government. It's clear they are avoiding contact at any meaningful level."

"What do you have, Admiral?" The President asked.

Chief of Staff Tully said, 'Mister President, we have calls backing up from virtually every head-of-state. You will need to respond as soon as possible. I suggest a priority that would consist of first the British Prime Minister, then --"

"Excuse me, Mister President, these reports coming in are more pressing," Admiral O'Brien interrupted.

"Go ahead, Admiral."

"We have reliable reports from U.S. military personnel in Israel that there have been major explosions in at least three cities. It's not clear what the targets were, but there appears to be high levels of radiation at the source of the explosions."

"Goddamnit, Admiral, what does that mean?" The President asked.

Admiral O'Brien hesitated, unsure if the intelligence supported the conclusion. "Mister President, it appears that Israel has sustained an attack of radiological weapons, so-called dirty bombs."

"What cities? What are the casualties?" The President asked.

"There were explosions in Tel Aviv, Haifa, and Beersheba. We don't know the casualty count, but that is not the real impact. We don't have specifics yet, but our experts estimate casualties by radiation poisoning could reach into the thousands in these urban areas. There's no antidote or any real treatment. Worse yet, the contaminated area will be uninhabitable for decades."

"Who?" was all the President could manage.

Helen Gladding answered, "Most likely the Syrians or Iranians working through one of their sponsored Palestinian groups."

Daniel Kolinski interjected, "It is probable that these are missing Soviet era bombs that have been missing from Moldova for some time."

"Moldova? Where is that?" The President asked.

"Between Romania and the Ukraine, Sir," Kolinski answered. "These bombs, fitted to rockets had been under guard by thousands of Russian troops for years. They were actually in the Trans-Dniester region, which has separatist ambitions. Slavs versus Romanians. Forty bombs have been missing for several years. The intelligence comes from actual Russian military records."

"Christ. I've never heard of Trans-Dniester. So what happened to these bombs?" The President asked.

"It would appear that they got into militant Muslim hands. Probably sold by Russian military officers, but we have no real evidence of that," Kolinski said.

"Academic issue now," Secretary Mueller said. "And the Israelis? What are they doing?"

"Just a moment, Sir," Admiral O'Brien said as an aide spoke to him.

"Mister President, the Israelis have launched a large number of aircraft that have already entered Syrian airspace. We're tracking several other squadrons flying east. That could only be Iraq or Iran. Since we're still in Iraq, we think they're headed for Iran."

For the next several minutes the senior staff of the United States government sat in silence. All were absorbed in their own thoughts. They watched the display board with the new symbols representing the Israeli threat without comment. A bright red icon flashed over Syria.

"Mister President, what we just saw was Damascus being hit with a nuclear weapon," Admiral O'Brien said. "We don't know what magnitude."

"Mother of God." The President said.

O'Brien continued, "Mister President, we have to assume that Tehran is next. We'll know in about an hour."

Attempts to make contact with the Israeli prime minister over the next hour were not successful. Inevitably, Admiral O'Brien reported the worst.

Tehran had been struck with two nuclear warheads.

Day three, Thursday 5:25 AM, White House Situation Room, Washington, D.C.

Away from the Situation Room conference table, Fielding said to Daniel Kolinski, "The fucking world never changes. The United States, the only super-power is absolutely impotent. There's not a goddamn thing we can do. All the major nuclear powers, the British, the French, the Chinese; all unable to stop a nuclear war by these Mickey Mouse states. And the fucking Russians; they don't know if they're on foot or horseback. The whole concept of deterrence needs to be rethought."

"Christ, deterrence? Genie's definitely out of the bottle. The mystique of nuclear warfare is gone. It's just a big-ass piece of ordinance now. Every asshole regime will want one. What the hell kind of deterrence can there be?" Kolinski said.

"Mister President," Admiral O'Brien said, "We have another development."

Everyone returned to the conference table.

"It's the North Koreans. They're crossing the DMZ in force. Heavy bombardment of Seoul."

The President murmured, "This can't be happening."

"Our forces, Admiral?" Secretary Mueller asked.

"Engaged, Sir. Heavily engaged."

"What can we do?" The President asked to no one in particular.

Carter Fielding suddenly stood up and addressed the President. "There is only one thing we can do, Mister President. Use nuclear weapons against the North Koreans. There is no other way we can counter them militarily. They outnumber our forces ten to one. It was always going to come to this if they ever attacked the South. No one ever thought they'd be desperate or stupid enough to do it."

Fielding could hardly believe he was recommending such a thing. His whole professional compass had been destroyed. There was no place left for diplomacy. The world had truly gone mad. Everything he had done in government seemed irrelevant now. The twenty-first century was already beginning to surpass the twentieth in horror.

Secretary Mueller said, "Doctor Fielding is correct. Our forces will quickly be overrun. There are no other options, Mister President. We must attack the Koreans immediately and decisively."

The President looked around the table. All reluctantly nodded affirmatively. The Pentagon Joint Chiefs added their agreement.

"This is unbelievable," The President said. With his face resting in both hands, he asked, "What do we do next, Admiral?"

Admiral O'Brien said, "I believe you know General Sloan, Sir. He is the most familiar with our strategic nuclear capabilities. General."

Lieutenant General Alexander Sloan's image appeared on one of the Situation Room monitors. He began to layout the status of the United States' nuclear deployment, followed by the various options distilled through years of war-gaming scenarios related to a North Korean invasion of the South.

A dazed President Benson was coached in making the requisite calls to the key heads-of-state with Helen Gladding's assistance. The conversation with the Chinese Premier was the most contentious.

The Army Major, current custodian of the 'football', assisted the President in the elaborate mechanics of electronically identifying the Commander-in-chief. Once identification was confirmed, the Major read the instructions by which the President would issue and authenticate the nuclear launch codes to the appropriate military commands.

The Major's voice cracked as he read out the instructions. The President typed the appropriate keys into the computer then sat down heavily.

On Friday, at 08:20 GMT, ballistic missiles, armed with Mk4 thermonuclear warheads were launched from two United States Trident II class submarines. Pre-defined attack plan *NK3-X* was designed to effect the complete annihilation of North Korean military capabilities and centers of government.

World War III had either ended or was just beginning.

THE END